Especially For Girls®
Presents

The KIDNAPPING of COURTNEY VAN ALLEN & What's-Her-Name

by Joyce Cool

ALFRED A. KNOPF · NEW YORK

This book is a presentation of Especially for Girls™,
Weekly Reader Books. Weekly Reader Books offers
book clubs for children from preschool through high school.
For further information write to: **Weekly Reader Books,**
4343 Equity Drive, Columbus, Ohio 43228.

Edited for Weekly Reader Books and published by
arrangement with Alfred A. Knopf, Inc.
Especially for Girls and Weekly Reader are trademarks of
Field Publications.

This is a Borzoi Book
Published by Alfred A. Knopf, Inc.

Library of Congress Cataloging in Publication Data
Cool, Joyce. The kidnapping of Courtney Van Allen
and what's-her-name.
Summary: When 12-year-old Jan Travis is kidnapped
along with her world-famous, wealthy friend, the
kidnappers demand something other than money.
[1. Kidnapping—Fiction]   I. Title.
PZ7.C776Ki 1981   [Fic]   80-28455
ISBN 0-394-84822-5   ISBN 0-394-94822-X (lib. bdg.)

one

OR my twelfth birthday my
Aunt Harry gave me a one-thousand-dollar bill, a
ten-foot-long boa constrictor named Calvin, and a
five-year diary. My Aunt Harry decided that the
thousand dollars would be deposited in the bank to
go toward my college education. To help ensure
that I lived to reach college age, Calvin would be
deposited in the zoo. I got to keep the five-year
diary.

Aunt Harry is really my father's Aunt Harriet
and, therefore, my great-aunt. She is what my
father describes as "off her rocker," and my mother
describes as "eccentric."

Every year, for as long as I can remember, my
parents and I have come to New York for one week
to visit my Aunt Harry. We always stay exactly one

week. My father calls this his "Aunt Harriet tolerance limit" and says that if we stayed even one more day past a week, he'd go crazy. This year, because my parents had to be in Europe, I was to stay with Aunt Harry for two weeks.

This is also the first year I've celebrated my birthday twice—on my actual birthdate and two days later. The reason for this is simple: My birthday is August 10, which was last Wednesday. And as every American citizen who ever watches television or reads the newspaper knows, on August 10, Courtney Van Allen and I (known to the masses as "What's-her-name") were kidnapped!

Maybe I'd better start from the beginning. . . .

We had landed at Kennedy International Airport and were in a taxi heading west on the Long Island Expressway toward Manhattan when my mother again expressed some doubt about leaving me with Aunt Harry. "Ben, I'd feel so much better about this trip if we were taking Jan with us."

"We've been all through that a dozen times, Susan," my father said. "This isn't a vacation, it's a conference. I've got to attend meetings and lectures. We're both expected to be present at various social functions. There's just no way we can take Jan with us."

"I know. It's just that I'm going to miss her so much." She reached over and stroked my hair. "Jan,

4

honey, you're sure you won't mind staying with Aunt Harriet for the next two weeks?"

"Mom," I reassured her, "I like Aunt Harry. I always have fun when I'm with her."

"That's sure more than I can say." My father grinned over at me.

"Ben—" My mother shot a frown in his direction meant to silence any more talk like that about Aunt Harry, but since she privately agreed with him, she couldn't help breaking into a smile.

My parents really love Aunt Harry, but I'm the one that's the closest to her. I don't think most people can see the hint of laughter and the warmth disguised behind Aunt Harry's unconventional behavior and sparkling brown eyes. But I can, and because I can, we have a special relationship.

I took my mother's hand. "I'll miss you a lot, but I'll be fine."

As it turned out, only the first half of that sentence proved to be true. But, of course, at that time none of us could have known what was going to happen to me in the next few days, not even the kidnappers, who were probably at that very moment making final plans to snatch Courtney Van Allen from her grandmother's penthouse.

The taxi drove into Manhattan and, as always, I peered out the window trying to see the tops of the skyscrapers.

A lot of people don't like New York City. They say

it's dirty and crowded and noisy. But I don't agree with them. Well, maybe it is—kind of dirty and sort of crowded—and a little noisy—but it's still the best city in the world to me.

I can leave Aunt Harry's apartment and within ten minutes be at a Broadway play, a movie, a museum, or even a zoo. I can row a boat, bicycle, horseback ride, or play tennis in Central Park.

Just about my favorite thing to do in New York is what I get to do the least: ride the subway. The subway is an underground train. There are hundreds of subway tunnels dug out under New York City, and they lead to most sections of the city. The train shakes and rattles down the track at a tremendous speed as the wind comes whistling in the windows and the lights flicker off and on. I seldom get to ride on the subway because I'm not allowed to go on it by myself, and for some reason adults don't seem to enjoy traveling around the city that way.

I'm not saying I'd want to trade where I live—which is in northern California on the Monterey Peninsula—with New York, but when it comes to visiting a city, give me New York every time.

By swearing and honking the horn for about five straight minutes, the cab driver managed to maneuver the taxi between about a dozen other yellow cabs and into the right-hand lane. He pulled up to the curb right in front of Aunt Harry's apartment building.

Once, when I was much younger, I asked Aunt Harry why her apartment was named the Fifth Avenue Central Park Tower. Even though I was only seven at the time, I could see she thought I was retarded. She explained it was so named because it was a tall building like a tower that was located on Fifth Avenue across from Central Park.

A doorman helped us from the taxi. It took several minutes for the cab driver, the doorman, and my father to unload our luggage from the trunk.

The Fifth Avenue Central Park Tower is protected by heavy security. No stranger goes anywhere in the building without first checking with the guard at the main desk in the lobby. There are rows of closed-circuit TV sets built into the panels behind the desk. By glancing at the rows of screens, the guard can check to see if everything is O.K. He can check in every elevator and in very corridor in the entire building.

My father told the guard that Mrs. Harriet Petrie was expecting us. The guard dialed Aunt Harry's apartment, nodded at the voice on the other end of the line, and motioned us toward the elevator.

Aunt Harriet lives on the twenty-third floor. The elevator travels one floor per second. During the entire twenty-three-second trip I kept my eyes glued on the TV camera bolted to the ceiling. I knew the guard in the lobby would be watching us on one of the TV screens behind his desk, and so I felt like waving or sticking my tongue out or something. I decided to stare into the camera without blinking for twenty-three seconds.

When the elevator door opened, Aunt Harry was there to greet us. "Darlings!" First she threw her arms around my father. "Ben, my sweet! It's so good to see you!"

My mother's turn came next. "Susan—angel! Let me look at you—as lovely as ever."

Then Aunt Harry turned her full attention to me. "And Jan." She walked slowly around me, carefully inspecting me from head to toe. Aunt Harry is a very tall woman. She folded her arms and peered down at me for what seemed like about three days. "Hmm, well, you seem to be growing out of that awful awkward stage—thank God!" She wrapped an arm around me and started to lead us toward her open apartment door. "Jan, my pet, I do believe there is still some hope for you to grow up to look as lovely as your mother."

I guess that was supposed to be some kind of a compliment. I glanced at my mother, who winked at me. That was her way of telling me she liked me even in my awkward stage.

Most people say nice things about the way I look. I have long, dark hair and blue eyes, but it's my smile that usually gets the most attention. Aunt Harry tucked a finger under my chin and made me look up at her. The instant our eyes met I could tell that she very much approved of me and my appearance.

The four of us had no more than walked through the apartment door when three of us—Aunt Harry was the exception—took an automatic step backward.

"Why, whatever is the matter?" Aunt Harriet asked.

She seemed surprised at our sudden reluctance to accompany her farther until she followed the wide-eyed, alarmed stare of three pairs of eyes. Our attention was focused on a wild jungle beast stretched out comfortably on Aunt Harry's long white sofa.

My father answered first. "My God, Aunt Harriet, what is that?"

"Ben," she replied calmly, "you're an intelligent, well-traveled man of the world. I see no reason why you should fail to recognize a jaguar when you see one."

"I recognize them when I see them in the zoo—behind bars."

"Miranda is too precious to put behind bars," Aunt Harry said indignantly.

"Miranda!" My father said the word in a disgusted voice and muttered a few other words under his breath.

"Yes, Miranda. Now don't stand there looking foolish. All of you, come in—and close the door behind you. Miranda is perfectly harmless."

At home we have two enormous Saint Bernard dogs. I'll bet Miranda could swallow both of them in a single gulp.

Aunt Harry went over to the sofa and lovingly stroked Miranda's silky yellow-and-black coat. As she caressed Miranda's whiskered face with her cheek, one of her long earrings dangled in front of the cat's yellow eyes. "As you know, I spent most of the winter months on my ranch in Brazil. It was there that I found Miranda. Poor stray little kitten." She kissed Miranda behind an ear. "She just wandered in from the jungle one morning. She's still not fully grown. She's my baby. Aren't you, sweetheart?" she asked Miranda.

Miranda didn't reply.

Out of respect for Aunt Harry's "kitten," my parents and I sort of tiptoed into the living room. We managed to find three seats that put the most possible distance between us and Miranda, who was now fondly licking Aunt Harry's face with a pink tongue the size of a skateboard.

"Aunt Harriet." My father choked, cleared his throat, and started again. "Aunt Harriet, there are laws against keeping wild animals in the middle of New York City. I mean, having Miranda here is against the law."

"Whoever made that ridiculous law obviously had a blind prejudice against all jaguars," Aunt Harry informed him.

"Please, Aunt Harriet, try to understand my point of view. Susan and I are leaving the day after tomorrow. We're going to be gone for two weeks. During that time we'd like to feel secure in the knowledge that our only child is being properly cared for."

"Benjamin, I am shocked!" Aunt Harry was shocked. "You know I adore Jan. I would never allow any harm to come to her."

"I know *you* wouldn't, Aunt Harriet, but I'm not so certain about Miranda. It would be different if we had several children. Then Miranda could eat one or two, and Susan and I wouldn't make a big fuss about it. But it happens we have only Jan, and before we leave we want to know she'll still be in one piece when we return."

It was always fun to watch the battle of wits that inevitably took place whenever my father and Aunt Harry got together. This time it appeared that Aunt Harry was giving in.

"Very well." She gave a resigned shrug and picked up the bell on the coffee table to summon the housekeeper. "I'll have Katie take Miranda to her room."

"Her room?" My mother spoke for the first time since laying eyes on Miranda. "Miranda has a room of her own?"

"Certainly. This is a large apartment, Susan. The least I can do is offer sanctuary to a few South American animals whose species face extinction."

"Are you saying you have more than one jaguar here?" my father asked.

"No, Miranda is the only jaguar."

I was surprised when my father let the subject drop with what was an evasive answer if ever I heard one. She had told him she had only one *jaguar*. She never said she didn't have other animals. I wisely said nothing.

Katie came into the room with a leash for Miranda. I'd say Katie is about the same age as Aunt Harry, which is about sixty. But, unlike Aunt Harry, Katie doesn't dye her hair, practice yoga, or buy her clothes at Bergdorf Goodman, so she looks quite a bit older.

I've known Katie all my life because she worked for Aunt Harry long before I was born. She shook hands with my mother and father, who greeted her warmly.

"Hi, Katie." I grinned up at her from where I sat.

"Jan, I'm so happy to hear you're going to stay for a while." She patted my hair in a sort of grandmotherly way.

People have done that for as long as I can remember. It makes me feel like a dumb little kid or a pet animal. But I liked Katie and really didn't mind too much.

"Now," she said to Aunt Harry. "I'm supposing you rang to have me escort Miranda to her room."

"Katie is the most intuitive woman I've ever known," Aunt Harriet marveled.

"It doesn't take much intuition, Mrs. Petrie. Within five minutes after guests arrive, I always take Miranda to her room—sometimes even sooner than that."

The rest of the day was fairly uneventful except for the after-dinner conversation. Everything had been perfectly normal during dinner. I like eating in Aunt Harry's dining room because there are floor-to-ceiling Victorian windows that look out over Central Park. It wasn't quite dark yet, just dusk, and while the adults were talking, I was admiring the view and, I guess, sort of daydreaming.

My parents and Aunt Harry were sipping coffee and discussing politics and the general bad state of world affairs when Aunt Harry got up to go over to the buffet. She reached inside a large silver box for what I naturally assumed was going to be a cigarette. Aunt Harry always smoked extra-long king-sized cigarettes in her extra-long jeweled cigarette holder. She returned to the table and lit up the longest, skinniest, pinkest CIGAR I've ever seen. I'll bet it was a foot long.

"What in God's name is that?" my father demanded to know.

"Ben, I've had about enough of your criticism for one day," Aunt Harry informed him, I guess referring to the remarks he had made earlier about Miranda.

It was interesting to hear Aunt Harry talk to my father in the same tone and using the same words

13

that he reserved for me whenever he didn't approve of something I'd said or done.

"I'm sorry, Aunt Harriet," he apologized, "but I thought you smoked only cigarettes."

"I'm surprised at you, Ben. You, of all people, after years in medical school, not aware that cigarette smoking is hazardous to one's health. It's written on every package: 'Warning: The Surgeon General has determined that cigarette smoking is dangerous to your health.'"

"I realize that, but—"

"Well, I simply decided not to take any chances. That's why I switched. I'd rather switch than drop dead."

I laughed, and Aunt Harry nodded her approval of my approval of her joke.

"And so I've given up cigarettes for Barkletts."

"Barkletts?" Three voices repeated the word in unison.

"That is correct. A Barklett"—she held the long, pink cigar out at arm's length for our inspection —"is made from the twigs of the rare peewee tree found only in the Amazon. The twig is hollowed out and filled with cured peewee bark. It is then wrapped in bright pink leaves that also come from the peewee tree."

"Has it occurred to you, Aunt Harriet, that the rare South American peewee may face extinction if many people take up smoking Barkletts?"

Aunt Harry ignored the sarcasm of my father's question and said, "Believe me, few people can afford to smoke Barkletts. They are very expensive. I limit myself to two a day. On very special occasions I sometimes allow myself three Barkletts a day."

Aunt Harry reached for the silver candlestick near her end of the table. She held the lighted candle beneath the tip of her Barklett, drew in her breath, and leaned back luxuriously in her velvet-covered chair. "In these inflationary times, I've found it necessary to give up so many of life's small pleasures."

My father looked across the table at my mother. They were both trying hard not to smile. "What have you had to give up, Aunt Harriet?" my dad asked.

Aunt Harry puffed at her cigar, and a trace of a coffee aroma filled the air. Most cigars make me sick, but Aunt Harry's Barklett smelled delicious.

"For one thing," she said, "my stock of vintage wine. It's up to fifty-six dollars a bottle now. When your Uncle M was living, it was only nineteen dollars, and we had a bottle every evening with dinner. I'm comfortably rich, but unless one is a Van Allen, one does feel the pinch of the times."

I knew Aunt Harry was referring to Isabelle Van Allen, who also lived in the Fifth Avenue Central Park Tower. Whenever there is a discussion about rich people, the name Van Allen is bound to be mentioned. The Van Allens are one of the wealthiest families in the world.

My mother breathed in the coffee scent that now pleasantly floated about the room. "Aunt Harriet, I have to admit that Barkletts smell wonderful. May I ask how much you pay for them?"

My mother's curiosity seemed to have gotten the better of her. Had I asked the same question, I would have been told that it was impolite to ask someone how much things cost.

"Each Barklett costs five dollars. I have a fresh case of one hundred shipped to me each month."

I did some fast mental arithmetic and calculated that Aunt Harry spent five hundred dollars a month on Barkletts. Also, I figured that she smoked three Barkletts a day more often than she'd admitted.

"I'd be happy to offer you a Barklett," Aunt Harry said generously, "but I know neither of you smoke. How about you, Jan, my pet? Would you care to try a Barklett?"

"Aunt Harriet!" The protest came from both my parents.

Aunt Harry flashed a devilish smile at them. "Teasing, darlings, just teasing. You may depend on one thing"—she took a long puff on the weird pink twig from the peewee tree—"your child shall be protected by me from Miranda and Barkletts."

Later that night, after I had slipped into bed and

was just reaching to turn off the light, Aunt Harry came in to say good night.

"Jan, my pet, I want you to get a good night's sleep because I have a surprise for you. Tomorrow I'm going to take you to the penthouse and introduce you to Courtney Van Allen."

two

"**C**OURTNEY Van Allen—imagine that!" My mother had just learned of Aunt Harry's surprise. "And you're going to meet her, Jan. Why, I think that's very exciting. Do you realize that she's probably the best-known twelve-year-old in the country, maybe even in the world?"

I took a large gulp of orange juice to wash down the toast that was stuck in my throat. I was having a lot of trouble swallowing everything that morning, which was a sure sign that I was nervous.

It's true, Courtney Van Allen's name and face is known to every man, woman, and child in the United States. Her grandfather owns a car factory in Detroit. The latest sport model manufactured by the Van Allen Company is called the "Courtney," named after you-know-who. Her maternal grandparents own the largest cereal company in America. When Courtney was two years old, they named what became their most popular cereal after her, "Courtney Crummies." Her baby picture is still on every box of Crummies.

Courtney's mother is just about the best-known actress in Hollywood. She's so famous that when anyone even says the initials SS, you know they're talking about Sylvia Sutton.

For the past three years, every Thursday night at eight o'clock, I've watched "The Sylvia Sutton Show" on television. It's all about this beautiful, brilliant blond reporter (played by Sylvia, of course) who manages each week to solve an important mystery and write a scoop story for her newspaper before the entire LA police force and every other reporter in the city even know what's going on.

Hardly a day goes by that you don't see James Van Allen's picture in the paper. Courtney's father is a United States senator. A lot of people believe he's planning to run for President someday.

The more I thought about meeting Courtney Van Allen, the more I lost my appetite.

"Jan, eat your breakfast."

"Mom, I can't." I toyed about with the corners of my napkin. "I've never met anyone famous before. What will I say?"

"Honey, she's no different from anyone else. Just talk to her the same way you do the rest of your friends."

"That's right, she's no different," my father said. "The only difference between you and Courtney Van Allen is that she has a movie star mother, a father who—God help us all—will probably become President one day, her picture plastered on those crummy Courtney Crummies stored in thousands of cupboards in homes all over the nation, and maybe twenty million dollars in the bank. So relax, Jan. With all you two have in common, you're sure to get along just fine."

"Dad, was that supposed to make me feel better?"

My father laughed and reached over and squeezed my hand. "I'm sorry, honey. Do you want to know what I really think? I'll bet that Courtney Van Allen, after staying at her grandmother's apartment for a while, is dying to have the company of someone her own age."

"Do you really think so?" I asked, my hopes rising.

He nodded. "Yes, I do. You follow your mother's advice. Just be yourself and act around Courtney Van Allen the same way you act around your friends at home. O.K.?"

"O.K.," I agreed.

Aunt Harry set her coffee cup down with a bang and stated emphatically, "There is absolutely no reason in the world why a niece of mine should feel inferior to Courtney Van Allen—or anyone else for that matter. You remember this, Jan Travis, you are à bright, charming girl"—a compliment from Aunt Harry! I could hardly believe it!—"and you'll be doing Mrs. Van Allen a favor if you can make friends with her granddaughter."

"Why? I'd think someone that rich and famous would have lots of friends already."

"Money and fame, my dear, do not necessarily guarantee friendship. Since Courtney has come to live with her grandmother, I think she has been a very lonely child."

My father said, "According to the *New York Times*, after her parents' separation, she was living with her mother."

My mother said, "According to the latest issue of *Newsweek*, Courtney has been living with her father."

I said, "According to the *Weekly Reader*, Courtney has been living at a private girl's school in Switzerland."

Aunt Harry said, "This afternoon, my pet, you can find out all about Courtney Van Allen, according to Courtney Van Allen."

The Van Allen penthouse occupied the entire top floor of the Fifth Avenue Central Park Tower.

A butler greeted us at the door. "Good afternoon, madam, miss. Mrs. Van Allen is expecting you. She will see you in her bedroom. If you will follow me, please."

Aunt Harry and I wordlessly trailed behind the

butler as he led us down a long corridor. I felt like I was inside a museum. The walls were covered with paintings and heavy tapestries. There were several tables on either side of the hallway. On the tables were vases of different sizes and shapes and a few ancient-looking statues.

The butler stopped in front of a dark wood paneled door. He knocked once, opened the door, and led us inside.

"Mrs. Van Allen," he spoke to a lady seated in the middle of the most gigantic bed I'd ever seen, "Mrs. Petrie and her niece are here to see you."

"Thank you, Raymond. That will be all." Mrs. Van Allen turned to Aunt Harry. "Mrs. Petrie, it's good to see you again. And I'm so delighted you could bring your niece—"

"Jan," Aunt Harry said.

"Yes," Mrs. Van Allen continued, "Jan. Won't you both please sit down?" She waved us toward two chairs near the bed. "Please forgive me. I'm usually up by one, but I'm a little slow getting around today."

I glanced at a clock on the mantel and saw that it was nearly two o'clock.

Mrs. Van Allen was propped up in bed, a silver breakfast tray over her knees. I noticed there were no Courtney Crummies on the tray. Mrs. Van Allen had much better taste. She was about halfway through a delicious serving of eggs Benedict. She dabbed daintily at the corner of her mouth with an initialed napkin. She was wearing five different rings. If she wore that much jewelry in bed, I wondered what she'd look like dressed and out of bed.

I'd say she was about fifty-five or sixty years old. In order to disguise what was probably ordinary gray hair, she had had it dyed an odd shade of silvery pink. It was hard to tell with the sheets pulled up around her, but I don't think she was fat, just sort of pink and puffy.

"Can I get either of you something to drink?" she asked.

"No, thank you," said Aunt Harry.

Aunt Harry and I had just eaten lunch. We had had breakfast five hours ago.

Mrs. Van Allen smiled at me. "Well, as I was saying, er . . ."

"Jan," I said.

"Yes, Jan. As I was saying, I was overjoyed to hear there was to be another girl the same age as Courtney in the building. I'm afraid the poor child hasn't been too happy living here with me. I hope you two will get along well together and perhaps even become good friends. Would you like to meet Courtney now?"

I nodded and said that I would.

Mrs. Van Allen picked up the phone and dialed one number. "Denise, would you come in here one moment, please?"

A few minutes later, a very thin, pale woman

wearing dark horn-rimmed glasses entered.

"Denise, I'd like you to meet Mrs. Petrie and her niece, er . . ."

"Jan," I repeated. I had always considered my name to be all right as names go. I mean, it wasn't one of the really great names like Leslie or Kelly, but it wasn't awful either, like Gertrude or Myrtle. And until now I had always thought it was an easy name to remember.

"Yes, Jan. Denise is Courtney's governess," she explained. "She will take you to meet Courtney."

"Jan," Aunt Harry said as I started to follow Denise out of the room, "I'll be running along soon, but you stay as long as you wish."

"All right, Aunt Harry." I smiled politely to Mrs. Van Allen. "Good-bye, Mrs. Van Allen."

"Good-bye, er . . ."

"Jan," I said.

"Yes, good-bye, Jan. I hope we'll be seeing you again soon."

Mrs. Van Allen seemed like a nice enough lady, but I was beginning to suspect that she had a poor memory.

On the way to Courtney's room Denise asked, "What is your last name, Jan?"

"Travis," I replied.

"Will you be staying with your aunt long?"

"I'll be here about two weeks. Just while my parents are in Europe."

"Good." She nodded curtly. "Maybe you can help take Courtney off my hands for a while."

I thought that was a funny remark for a governess to make. I wasn't sure how to respond, so I didn't say anything.

Courtney had the kind of bedroom every girl dreams about. The walls were a soft pink. The carpet was a deeper shade of pink. Against one wall, near the center of the room, was a canopied bed covered with frilly pink-and-white lace.

At first glance I noticed a portable color TV set, a stereo, and about forty stuffed animals. On either side of the fireplace were tall glass cases containing what had to be the world's greatest doll collection.

On the far wall there were windows looking out over Central Park. Beneath the windows was a window seat covered with pink-and-white cushions. To the right of the windows was a bookcase. Just in front of the bookcase was a desk. Seated at the desk was Courtney Van Allen. She was playing solitaire. Her eyes remained fixed on the cards in front of her.

"Courtney, this is Jan Travis. Jan is staying with her aunt on the twenty-third floor."

Courtney continued to play solitaire. She carefully moved a red ten onto a black jack, a red seven onto a black eight, and covered the seven with a black six before she looked up at me. She inspected me about as carefully as she had the cards.

"Hi," I said.

My mother and I both have dark hair and blue eyes and sort of a light sprinkle of freckles across our noses. So when people sometimes tell me they think I'll grow up to look like my mother, I believe them. I don't know if anyone ever tells Courtney they think she'll grow up to look like her mother, but if they do, they're lying. Courtney resembles Sylvia Sutton about as much as a mouse resembles a Siamese cat.

I've seen a lot of pictures of Courtney in magazines and newspapers, not even counting the millions of Courtney Crummies cereal-box pictures. The last picture I remember seeing was the one in the *Weekly Reader* taken at a girl's school in Switzerland. In it she had been wearing a riding outfit: a red jacket, pants, and boots. She had looked healthy, tanned, happy, and—clean. The caption under the picture had been *Courtney Van Allen, astride Lightning Charlie, wins first prize in jumping contest*.

Now Courtney was wearing a dirty, beat-up T-shirt about three sizes too big. It had a hole in the sleeves and two more in the back. On the front, in large letters, were the words *Drop Dead*. The faded blue jeans she wore had about twenty patches all over them, and embroidered on one leg, just under the knee, were the words *I said Drop Dead*.

Her feet were bare except for both big toes. On one of her big toes she was wearing a pearl ring. A ring shaped like a snake was coiled around the other big toe. Her stringy blond hair was held back with what looked like an Indian headband.

Could this really be the girl who had everything? Except for the rings, she looked like a war orphan.

While I was recovering from the shock of meeting the real Courtney Van Allen, Denise was saying, "I'll leave you two girls alone to get acquainted."

Both of us watched Denise walk from the room. Neither of us said anything. I wanted to say something, but I couldn't think of anything to say. I didn't think I should say, "Do you know you look like a war orphan?" So I just stood there looking down at her game of solitaire.

Courtney walked around the desk and stood next to me. She stared me straight in the eye and said in a low voice, "You think I look weird, don't you?"

"No," I lied.

"Yes, you do," she said, raising her voice. "Well, I look this way because I've decided to become a dropout."

"Why?" I asked.

"Why?" She shouted the word as if she thought I was crazy for asking such a question. "Why? Why? I'll tell you why! Because I'm sick! SICK! I'm sick of everything and everybody! That's why I'm wearing this message on my shirt. I've been wearing this shirt for forty-six straight days, and I'm going to keep right on wearing it until *certain* people get the message and drop dead!"

"What certain people?"

"My darn mother, my darn father, my darn grandmother, and that darn Denise! They all stink! STINK! They're rotten! They smell!"

She seemed to enjoy my surprised expression. "You'd probably get your mouth washed out with soap if you talked like that, wouldn't you?"

I knew I'd get a lot more than that.

"Well," she continued, "I won't. I can say anything and I can do anything I want."

She picked up the cards and tucked them neatly in their cardboard box. She carried the box of cards around to the side of the desk and dropped them into the wastebasket.

"Why are you throwing them away?"

"It's Monday, isn't it? Every Monday I get a new deck of cards. I never use the same deck for longer than one week. After one week, they start to stink, like everything else around here."

"If you're going to throw them away, could I have them?"

"It's all right with me if you want stinking cards."

I picked the box of cards out of the wastebasket.

"Where are you from, anyway?" Courtney asked.

"California," I replied.

For a minute I think Courtney forgot she was being tough. The word *California* sparked a genuine interest. "California. I used to live in California. We lived on a ranch in Encino. My mother still lives there—and my dog, Rhoda, and . . ." Her voice trailed off and she looked sad.

"Courtney, I was wondering, if your mother comes here to visit you sometime, could I meet her? I watch her show every week and—"

"I already told you how I feel about my mother. She stinks, and that dumb show of hers stinks. Anyway, she hasn't been here since June."

"June!" I repeated. "You haven't seen your mother for two months?"

"Actresses are busy people, you know. Besides, I'm not a baby. I don't need a mother to boss me around all the time."

"But don't you miss her?"

"No! I told you, she stinks!" Then she wanted to know, "Where are *your* parents?"

"They're leaving tomorrow for London. My father has to attend a conference there." I thought of my mother, who was practically having a nervous breakdown because she was leaving me for two weeks. I guess not all mothers love their children. Maybe Sylvia Sutton thinks Courtney stinks too. "I'm staying with my Aunt Harry until they get back."

"Your *Aunt* Harry?"

"When I was little," I explained, "I could only pronounce the first half of her name, which is Harriet. So I've called her Aunt Harry ever since."

Courtney said sarcastically, "I suppose your uncle's name is Mary?"

"No, he died before I was born. His name

was—" I stopped suddenly, remembering his name.

"Was what?"

"Uncle Mamm," I mumbled under my breath.

"What?"

"Uncle Mamm," I mumbled again.

"I didn't hear you."

I took a deep breath and said, "Uncle Marion."

"Uncle Marion!" Courtney gave a snort. "Aunt Harry and Uncle Marion!" She broke into wild cries of laughter.

If it hadn't been for her attitude, I would have had to admit they were pretty funny names, but instead I said defensively, "Marion is a man's name too, you know."

Courtney continued to laugh.

I decided it was time to change the subject. I spotted a book lying on the bed. "My class read this last year when I was in the sixth grade," I said, picking up the book.

"I just finished reading it," Courtney said. "I thought it was a neat book, did you?"

At last, I thought, something we can agree on. "Yes, I thought it was neat, too. My favorite part was when—"

"I liked it," she interrupted, "because it's about a girl who runs away from home—something I've been thinking about for a long time."

I was shocked. "You're thinking about running away?"

"Yes, and maybe to the same place *she* ran away to," Courtney said, referring to the character in the book.

"You mean the New York Metropolitan Museum of Art?"

"Of course. Don't you see, it's perfect. Nobody's ever thought about running away to the New York Metropolitan Museum of Art before, except the person who wrote that book. And what makes it really perfect is that the museum is just down the street." After a long pause, she added, "You can run away with me if you want to."

"Me—run away? My family would worry about me."

Courtney looked at me as if I were from some other planet. "What's wrong with you? Don't you know that's the whole point?"

"No, Courtney, I'm not running away." I could see she knew it was useless to try to persuade me to change my mind. "But I haven't been to the museum since I was here last year. Maybe we could go over together sometime, if you want to."

"O.K.," she agreed. "What about tomorrow morning?"

"My parents are leaving in the morning. I could go in the afternoon though."

Before I left it was agreed that Courtney would come down to Aunt Harry's and pick me up at one o'clock the following afternoon.

When I got back to Aunt Harry's, I found my

mother in the bedroom packing clothes. I went in, threw my arms around her, and hugged her tight.

"Hmm, what's this for?" she asked.

"It's because you are nothing, nothing, nothing like Sylvia Sutton."

"Honey, that's not much of a compliment. Every woman in the world would like to look like Sylvia Sutton."

"I'm talking about something a lot more important than looks," I said, still hugging her. "Anyway, you look ten times better than she does."

My mother laughed, planted a kiss on top of my head, and said, "Thank God, love is blind."

I sat down on the edge of the bed and watched her pack.

"Well, when do I get to hear all about the fabulous Courtney Van Allen?" she asked me.

"Mom, I think she's crazy."

"Jan, that's not a nice thing to say about someone."

"I'm not saying it to be mean. I'm saying it because I think she's crazy. You see these cards?" I held up the deck of cards I had rescued from the wastebasket. "She threw them away because it was Monday."

"What?" my mother asked in a puzzled voice.

"I'm not kidding. She thinks cards start to stink after a week. So every Monday she gets a new deck."

"Oh," she said, still obviously not understanding.

"She wears rings on her two big toes and signs on her shirt and pants telling everyone to drop dead. She wears a dirty Indian headband, and I don't think she's washed her hair for weeks. For the past forty-six days she's been a dropout."

"What do you mean, a dropout?"

"I—I'm not sure," I admitted. "I think she just doesn't want to belong to the establishment anymore. She says she's fed up with everything and everybody, so she's decided to become a dropout."

My mother carefully folded a slip. "That's all the world needs—a twelve-year-old dropout."

"She wants me to run away with her."

My mother stopped packing and gave me her undivided attention. "Jan, I'm not so sure you should see her again. The girl sounds like she's—"

I smiled and waited for her to say it.

"—crazy." My mother smiled back. She studied me for a moment, trying to decide whether or not she should let her daughter make friends with the richest, most famous, and maybe looniest girl in the world. "It doesn't sound like Courtney Van Allen will be a very good influence on you, but I think you're old enough not to let yourself be talked into anything foolish. You have a good mind, Jan. You've always been responsible and dependable, and I think it will take a lot more than a Courtney Van Allen to change that."

For the first time, I noticed a large, brightly wrapped package lying on the floor next to the bed. "What's that?" I asked.

"I wondered how long it would take you to spot that," she said, going back to her packing. "That's your birthday present."

"Really? Can I open it now?"

"No, you cannot."

"Who picked it out—you or Dad?"

"We picked it out together one day last week when we were able to ditch you for a few hours."

"Can I have three guesses?"

"No."

"Two guesses?"

"No."

"Mom, just one guess."

"No, no guessing."

I started to go over to have a closer look at the package.

"Jan, just stay where you are."

"Can't I even pick it up and sort of listen to the inside?"

"No."

"You and Dad won't be here for my birthday. When will I get to open it?"

"We're planning to call you Wednesday from our hotel. You can open it then." She pulled the lid down on the suitcase and snapped it shut. "Come on, my inquisitive young friend, let's see what your dad and Aunt Harry are up to, O.K.?"

We had just stepped into the hallway when we heard an ear-piercing scream that made our blood run cold. My mother and I grabbed for each other. The scream came a second time, if possible, louder than the first. My first thought was that there was a torture chamber hidden somewhere in the building and at that very moment someone was being tortured there.

My father came on the run, followed by Aunt Harry.

"Just stay calm," Aunt Harry shouted as she ran past us. "It's only Miranda. Ben," she yelled to my father, "open this door just a crack. Be ready to close it as soon as I give the word."

Unwrapping what looked like about ten pounds of raw hamburger, she nodded to my father to open the door. When it was opened about a foot, Aunt Harry took aim, wound up like a major league pitcher, and fired the meat into the room. My father didn't wait to be told to close the door. We all stood there, too weak from the experience to say anything.

Aunt Harry spoke first, trying to act as if nothing had happened. "My, it's warm this afternoon. That's New York in August for you. It's not so much the temperature as the humidity. I think we should all have a tall glass of iced tea."

When she brought us our drinks, I noticed I was the only one drinking iced tea. Everyone else was drinking a double martini.

"Aunt Harriet," my father was saying in his most serious tone, "Susan and I can't leave Jan here tomorrow if that animal stays."

"I know, Ben." Aunt Harry was equally serious. "I've called the zoo. Arrangements have been made for them to pick up Miranda sometime tomorrow."

My father gave her a grateful smile. "Thank you, Aunt Harriet."

"I knew it had to be done sooner or later. Miranda's a love, but she has been getting harder to handle lately. That meat was loaded with fifteen tranquilizers," she explained, "so Miranda will be drowsy for quite a while. I think you can all relax and rest easy now."

While the grown-ups were relaxing with their drinks, I leaned back and sipped my iced tea and thought about the fact that the day after tomorrow I'd be twelve years old.

I hadn't been looking forward to my birthday as much as usual because I'd be away from home and my parents and friends. But, I thought, I'd still be able to talk to my mother and father on the phone, and I'd have their present to open, so maybe it would be a good day after all. Boy, was I ever wrong!

three

COURTNEY came at exactly one o'clock. She was wearing the same "drop dead" outfit she had worn the day before and the forty-six days before that. The only difference was that she was sort of wearing tennis shoes. By "sort of" I mean the whole front part of both tennis shoes had been cut away so that her toes could stick out. She still wore rings on both of her big toes. But they weren't the same rings she had worn the day before.

"You have different rings on your toes," I observed out loud.

"Of course," Courtney replied simply. "These are my Tuesday rings. I wear different rings every day except for the weekend. On Saturday and Sunday I wear the same rings."

"Oh," I said. I was learning that Courtney could

say things that made absolutely no sense, but *the way* she said them made you *think* they made sense.

I took her into the living room to meet Aunt Harry. Aunt Harry was wearing a silk pants suit that looked like a pair of fancy pajamas. She was ready to go to her Tuesday afternoon bridge club party.

"I'm happy to meet you, Courtney. I must say you don't look much like those adorable little baby pictures I see on Courtney Crummies. I mean, you're still adorable, I'm sure, but you don't look—quite the same."

"Those pictures were taken when I was only two years old," Courtney explained, "and I hate them. And I hate Courtney Crummies. They stink! Take my advice, Mrs. Petrie, and NEVER eat them."

Aunt Harry didn't reply to this outburst. She stood silently and peered down at Courtney.

"My other grandfather named a car after me, but at least he didn't put my picture on it. Well, those cars stink too. Take my advice and NEVER ride in one."

Aunt Harry was now staring at Courtney with a definite look of disapproval, but she only said, "Well, children, have a good time at the museum. What time can I expect you back, Jan?"

"We should be back by three-thirty," I replied.

"We'll be back at thirteen and a half minutes after four," Courtney corrected me.

"Just so you're here when I get home. I'll be

back"—Aunt Harry stared straight at Courtney—
"at three and one-quarter minutes after five o'clock
P.M." She picked up her purse and patted my
cheek. "Jan, don't forget, don't go near that door."

As Courtney and I walked down the hallway
toward my bedroom, Courtney asked me, "What
did she mean by that?"

For some reason I liked Courtney's puzzled
expression better than her forty-seven-day-old
dropout one, so I pretended not to understand. "By
what?" I asked.

"You know, she told you not to go near some
door. What door?"

"Oh, that." We were just passing Miranda's door.
"She meant this door. That was my Uncle Marion's
workroom, a sort of laboratory where he worked on
strange experiments." I emphasized the word
strange.

Courtney's eyes widened. "What kind of experiments?"

"Don't worry about it, Courtney. As long as we
keep the door closed, we're safe."

By some marvelous coincidence, Miranda chose
that exact moment to let loose with one of her
blood-curdling screams. Courtney took off down the
hall like a bullet. I ran behind her, trying not to
laugh. When we got to my room, she slammed the
door shut and leaned all her weight against it to
keep the "experiment" from getting in. She had
gone pale with fright.

"O.K., Jan," her voice was quivering, "here's what we'll do. I'll hold the door. You go to the phone and call the police station and fire department and—the marines! Call the marines first. They have bigger guns than the police."

"There's no phone in here."

"A bedroom without a phone." Courtney stared at me in disbelief, then screamed at me in panic. "Well, how are we going to get out of here?"

I knew I should tell her the truth, but I was having so much fun, I couldn't. "Courtney, don't be afraid. Uncle Marion's mad monster usually calms down after eating ten pounds of raw hamburger."

"Monster!" she whispered the word. "Well, what he seems to want right now is ninety-five pounds of live meat."

"Don't be silly, Courtney. He hasn't eaten anyone in years. My aunt fed him before she left, so he should drop off to sleep any minute now."

While Courtney stood against the door, stunned, I tucked two dollars of my vacation fund money into my slacks pocket along with some loose change. "O.K., I guess I'm ready."

Courtney reluctantly left her post at the door and sank down on the bed. "We can't go yet."

"Why?"

"We have to wait for Denise. My grandmother insisted that she go with us."

"Doesn't your grandmother think you're old enough to go to the museum by yourself?"

"I'm never allowed to go anywhere by myself or with other kids unless there's a grown-up along with me."

"That sounds boring," I said.

"It's not only boring, it stinks."

"Why aren't you allowed to go out alone?"

"Because of the kidnap threats."

"Kidnap threats?" Now I was the one who felt scared. "Someone has threatened to kidnap you?"

"Someone," she repeated. "Ha! We've received dozens of threats. Ever since I was born, crazy people everywhere have threatened to kidnap me. It's not exactly easy being one of the richest kids in the world, you know."

I was beginning to think she had a point there. "What can Denise do if someone does try to kidnap you? Is she a karate expert or something?"

"Denise is so puny she couldn't karate-chop a fly." Courtney snorted. "She always carries a revolver in her purse."

There was a knock on the door, and we both jumped a foot. It was Katie.

"Your governess is waiting for you in the living room, Miss Van Allen," she informed Courtney.

Courtney ran so fast out the door and past Miranda's room that she almost mowed Katie down.

"My," Katie whispered to me, "she must really love her governess."

"No." I smiled. "As a matter of fact, she really thinks she stinks."

The first thing I looked at when I reached the living room was Denise's purse. Then I carefully looked at Denise. She didn't appear at all like somebody who would be carrying a revolver around with her. With her horn-rimmed glasses and her hair pulled back in an unattractive bun style, she reminded me of Mrs. Gray, who was my third-grade teacher.

She readjusted her glasses and hitched her purse strap over her shoulder. "Well, if you're ready, let's get going."

The walk to the museum took ten minutes, during which time Denise did not say one word. We stopped on the sidewalk just outside the entrance to the museum.

"Do we have the same deal today, Denise?" Courtney asked her.

"The same deal," Denise agreed. "I'll meet you here at four o'clock." Without any farewell, Denise abruptly turned and left.

"What do you mean, 'the same deal'?" I asked Courtney.

"Denise and I made a bargain about a month ago. She can leave me whenever she wants to, and I won't tell my grandmother; and I can leave her whenever I want to, and she won't tell my grandmother."

"Wouldn't she be fired if your grandmother found out?"

"Of course, but I'm not going to tell her. Denise

hates me and I hate her, but she's the only governess who ever agreed to let me go places by myself."

"She doesn't sound like a very good governess to me," I told Courtney.

"She isn't. She stinks. A good governess would stay with me all the time, but since I need my freedom, I pretend to my grandmother that I really like her. Well, where shall we go?" Courtney asked.

"What do you mean?" I stared at her. "We're here."

"Do you think I want to go into that boring place?" She pointed at the museum.

"I sort of like it."

"Well, I don't. We've got two and a half hours of FREEDOM. We can go anywhere, just so we're back here at four o'clock. For the last month, since my bargain with Denise, I've been riding the subway almost every day."

"Really? You ride the subway by yourself?"

"Sure. Let's go." Courtney started walking down the street.

"Wait a minute, Courtney. I'm not allowed to ride the subway by myself."

"So, you're not by yourself. You're with me."

"I know my parents wouldn't let me ride it without an adult along."

"You told me your parents left for London this morning."

"They did, but my Aunt Harry thinks we're

spending the afternoon at the museum. I know she wouldn't want me riding underground all around the city. Besides that, it's very easy to get mixed up on the trains down there. We might wind up anywhere in New York. Then what would we do?"

Courtney leveled a gaze at me. "I told you, I've ridden the subway plenty of times by myself. We WON'T get lost. There's NO WAY we can get lost."

It was the moment of decision for me. I could do what I knew was right and refuse, or I could do what was one of my favorite things in the world: ride the subway.

The only thing holding me back was my mother's last words to me that morning: ". . . and for heaven's sake, Jan, stay away from the door until Miranda's out of the apartment—and if you're going to spend any more time with Courtney, use your own good sense—and, honey, listen to Aunt Harriet—and—"

"Come on, Jan," Courtney urged.

My mother's words faded away.

"O.K., Courtney, maybe you're right. I mean, I am eleven years, three hundred and sixty-four days old—and I think that's old enough to ride on a subway by myself." I grinned. "Or at least with you."

Courtney grinned back as we headed down the street. "Eleven years, three hundred and sixty-four days old," she repeated. "Does that mean that your birthday is tomorrow?"

I nodded.

"Are you going to have a birthday party?"

"How can I? I don't know anyone in the whole city except Aunt Harry and you."

"You can invite me," Courtney suggested. "It would be a very intimate, exclusive party."

We walked for twenty minutes before we found a subway entrance. I was beginning to enjoy Courtney now that, temporarily at least, she had dropped her "dropout" act. We walked down two flights of stairs. I followed Courtney up to a window and bought a token. We stuck the token into a machine and walked through the turnstile out onto the station platform. On the opposite side of the tracks a train was just pulling out. A few minutes later a train sped down the tracks toward us.

"We'll take this train first," Courtney explained. "When it gets to the end of the line, we'll just walk over to the other side of the platform and take the opposite train back."

That sounded simple enough. If that was all there was to it, I didn't see why I hadn't been allowed to ride the train by myself a long time ago.

It took about forty minutes to reach the end of the line. During that time a lot of people made their way on and off the train. Most of them looked like very ordinary people, but a few looked weird and made me think about the kidnapping threats Courtney had mentioned.

When we reached the final stop, it was two-thirty. "We don't have to be back for an hour and a half," Courtney said. "Let's go up and see where we are."

"O.K.," I agreed. "Maybe we can find someplace to get a Coke."

When we reached ground level, we found we were in a rundown section of the city. The length of the block was covered with litter and trash lying in the gutters and on the sidewalks. We passed a few people sitting limply on the front stoops of their tenement buildings, hoping to get a little relief from the heat.

As we walked toward a corner drugstore Courtney said, "Ugh, am I glad we don't live here. Why do you suppose *anyone* lives here? I wonder why they don't move?"

"I don't know," I answered. "Maybe they don't have enough money to move."

We passed a group of kids playing jacks on the sidewalk. "Look at how they're dressed. They must really be poor," Courtney said sympathetically.

"Courtney, you're about the richest kid in the world, and *you're* dressed worse than they are."

"That's different. I don't *have* to dress this way."

Courtney's logic didn't make any sense to me, but I didn't say anything. We went inside the drugstore and sat down at the counter. We each ordered a Coke. We drank the Cokes quickly because we wanted to be back at the subway by three o'clock.

We were standing at the cash register waiting to

pay for the Cokes when Courtney said, a little frantically, "Jan, I can't find my money."

The lady behind the counter gave us a sour look. "Don't try to pull any of that stuff on me. You two don't leave here until I get eighty cents."

Courtney dug around in her jean pockets. She pulled the right pocket inside out and poked a finger through a small hole. "I'm sorry, Jan. The change must have dropped out."

"Listen, kid." The sour expression turned into a mean one. "All I know is that I want my eighty cents, and one of you better come up with it fast!"

"It's O.K.," I assured both of them. "I've got some money." I paid for the Cokes, and we hurried from the store.

"Do we still have enough money to buy our return tokens?" Courtney asked, sounding a little worried.

I counted my remaining change. "We can make it. We'll even have a nickel to spare."

We retraced our steps back to the subway entrance, hoping we might find some of Courtney's lost change. We didn't. Once inside the subway station, we bought two tokens and sat down on a bench to wait for the train to arrive.

"Courtney, how do you ever figure out which train to take?"

"Oh, it's nothing," she said proudly. "I just read one of those maps." She pointed to a wall behind us. The wall was painted with different-colored lines and numbers, representing all the train routes for the entire New York City subway system.

"You're pretty smart, Courtney. That map doesn't make any sense to me."

"Yes, I am smart," she agreed. "Maybe I can understand it better than you because I'm older."

I looked at her. "How old are you?"

"I was twelve in June."

"That was only two months ago. You call that older?"

"Well, what would you call it?" she wanted to know.

I gave her a disgruntled look and was still trying to think of a smart answer when we got on the train. We found two seats together.

Each time the train came to a stop, about three times as many people got on as got off. Before long, each seat and every available inch of floor space was covered with a body. We were packed so tightly together I was afraid I might smother to death.

"How many people are they going to let on?" I asked Courtney. All I could see was an elbow to the right of me and in front of me, a fat man's stomach poking me in the nose. I was beginning to feel like a sardine.

"I don't know," Courtney said, "but we get off at the next stop."

"How are we going to get off?"

"Just plow through. Stay right behind me."

The train came to a stop. I heard the doors open, but I couldn't move. I was pinned to my seat by a fat stomach that wouldn't budge. "Mister," I shouted up at the fat stomach, "I have to get out here." Still the fat stomach didn't move. "Mister," I shouted even louder, "please move. I have to get out here!" By this time I was desperate. I knew the doors would be slamming shut any second, and Courtney and I would be carried off to some strange place.

I guess Courtney was feeling desperate too. "O.K., Jan, this will move him. Just be ready to aim for the door." She cupped her hands around her mouth and screamed at the top of her lungs, "I'M GOING TO THROW UP!"

There were cries of alarm as Courtney began to gag. Suddenly, people began pushing and shoving to get out of our way. So we just squeezed through the parting crowd and out the door.

"Courtney," I said, "you are crazy!"

"It worked, didn't it?"

We ran quickly up the stairs to get out of the way of people who were still stumbling out of the train's opened doors.

When we reached the street level, I looked around for familiar sights. There weren't any. "Where are we?" I asked Courtney.

"I don't know," Courtney replied weakly.

"What?" I cried in shock.

"I don't know, Jan. I really don't know."

"What do you mean, you don't know?" I shouted.

"I mean," Courtney was turning pale, "I don't know."

"You're the one who told me we COULDN'T get lost. You said there was NO WAY we could get lost. Are you trying to tell me we're LOST?"

"We should be close to Fifth Avenue," Courtney said in what was not a very convincing voice. "We'll just have to walk a little farther, that's all."

We stood on the corner looking hopelessly one way and then another, trying to decide which direction to take.

I said, "In twenty minutes we're supposed to meet Denise back at the museum."

"Well, we'll be a little late, that's all." Courtney was trying not to sound too concerned. "Let's go into that store across the street and ask how far it is to Fifth Avenue."

We entered the store and found a clerk. "Excuse me," I said, "but could you tell us how to get to Fifth Avenue and the Metropolitan Museum of Art?"

"Fifth Avenue?" She said the words as though I had asked for directions to China. "It's at least an hour's walk from here."

"Then we'll run," Courtney said. "Just show us which way to go."

The clerk walked out on the sidewalk with us and pointed to her right. "Stay on this street and you'll reach Fifth Avenue. But it's quite a walk, girls. I don't recommend it."

"I told you, we're going to run," Courtney said, taking off down the street.

"Thank you," I called back over my shoulder as I took off after Courtney.

We ran for about ten minutes. Finally, when we couldn't run any longer, we leaned up against a building to catch our breath. "I guess—we'd better —walk for a while," Courtney wisely suggested, panting hard.

We walked for one hour and still no Fifth Avenue. "It's probably the next block," I said. It wasn't. We kept on walking. The time was now five o'clock. Aunt Harriet would just be getting home from her bridge club.

We walked for a long time before we decided to go into another store and ask how many more blocks we had to go. One of the customers came out and pointed to the left. "It's quite a walk, girls. At least an hour, I'd say."

Courtney and I stared at each other. "It can't be that way," Courtney declared. "We just came from that direction."

"Well, I'm sorry, young lady, but that's the way to Fifth Avenue all right," the man repeated, still looking to his left.

We started walking back the way we had come. "If only we had some money," Courtney said, "we could get on the right subway this time."

"Well, we don't have enough money, thanks to you," I snapped.

We dragged our feet along the pavement for another hour. "If we even had a dime we could call home and ask them to come pick us up," Courtney said.

"Well, we don't have even a dime, thanks to you," I snapped again.

"Then there's only one thing left to do," Courtney said sadly.

"What?"

"Turn ourselves in."

"You mean—go to the police station and tell them we're lost?"

"Of course." Courtney brightened a little at the idea. "They always let you have one free phone call."

We both remembered we had passed a police station the first time we had walked the street going in the opposite direction. We quickened our pace.

When we finally reached the station, we hesitated for a few minutes before getting up enough nerve to go inside.

Once inside the station, Courtney marched up to a policeman seated behind a very high desk. "Excuse me, sir. Could you tell me where the phone is? We'd like to make our one free phone call."

The policeman stopped writing, laid down his pen, and stared over the edge of his desk. "What free call?"

"The free call you let everybody make. You let

crooks make free calls—pickpockets, muggers, robbers—even murderers. I go to the movies, you know," Courtney informed him, "so I know you let everybody make one free call. Well, we want to make our free call. If you don't mind, we'd like to make it now."

"This is a police station, kid," the policeman said impatiently, "not a place for children to play. Now run along home."

"Play! Who said anything about playing?" Courtney shouted up at him indignantly. "We demand our rights. We want to make our one free phone call now."

I was beginning to wish Courtney would stop using the word *we*.

"I told you once to run along home," the policeman said in the same impatient voice.

"We've *been* running along home for three hours," Courtney screamed hysterically, "only we can't find it!" I think the policeman was as surprised as I was to see tears spring into Courtney's eyes. She quickly blinked them away.

"You mean you're lost?" he asked in a kinder voice.

"That's why we want to make a phone call," I explained. "We thought we could call Courtney's grandmother or my aunt, and they could come pick us up."

"I see," he said. "Give me the number and I'll make the call for you." Courtney gave him her grandmother's number. "Now I'd like your name, please."

"Jan Travis," I said.

"Courtney Van Allen," Courtney said.

The policeman had started to write our names down but paused when he heard Courtney's name. "Courtney Van Allen?" he repeated, "you're not *the* Courtney Van Allen?"

Courtney nodded.

"Well, I'll be—" He dialed the Van Allen's number. "Hello, this is Sergeant Drakers from the Fifty-second Precinct . . . yes . . . yes, madam . . . they're here . . . yes, they're both fine." He gave directions to the precinct. "Yes, I'll do that, Mrs. Van Allen . . . yes . . . all right. Good-bye, madam.

"Your grandmother has been very worried," he told Courtney. Looking at me he said, "Mrs. Van Allen said she was bringing your aunt along with her. She asked me to keep an eye on both of you until they get here."

Courtney and I sat on a bench facing the policeman in gloomy silence. We had a lot of time to think. The main thing that worried me was that maybe Aunt Harry wouldn't trust me anymore. Whenever I did something wrong at home and my parents punished me, I always knew they still loved me, but Aunt Harry is sometimes hard to figure out. I wasn't sure what her reaction was going to be.

We listened to the station clock tick off thirty long

minutes. The only time the policeman let us out of his sight was when we went to the bathroom.

They arrived at seven o'clock. We listened to the clicking of their heels in the hallway. Mrs. Van Allen and Aunt Harry marched immediately over to Courtney and me. They wore almost identical expressions, which let us know, in no uncertain terms, that they were not pleased with the whole situation. They spoke to the policeman for a minute, then motioned us to follow them outside.

The Van Allen limousine was parked in front of the station. The chauffeur held open the door while all four of us climbed into the back seat. Under normal circumstances I would have considered riding in a chauffeur-driven limousine an exciting experience, but now I was feeling too miserable to even think about it.

Aunt Harry was still wearing her bridge outfit. Mrs. Van Allen had on a long pink gown that sort of matched her pink-gray hair. I was surprised she'd wear a dress like that to the police station. Even people as rich as the Van Allens must have some everyday clothes.

Mrs. Van Allen was the first to speak. She glared at Courtney and said, "This little escapade of yours has made me late for a very important party." That explained the dress. "I've given Denise orders to talk to you when you get home about the dangers of running around the city by yourself."

I really wanted to apologize to Aunt Harry for all

the trouble I had caused. "Aunt Harry—"

"Silence!" she said in an icy tone. "We'll discuss this when we get home."

Courtney, Aunt Harry, and I were dropped off in front of the Fifth Avenue Central Park Tower. Mrs. Van Allen drove on to her party after asking Aunt Harry if she would ring Denise. Aunt Harry called her from the lobby.

When Denise arrived, she gave Courtney a dirty look and said, "You brat! Don't you have any sense at all?"

I noticed Aunt Harry's eyebrows raise slightly.

Maybe Denise noticed too, because she said in a somewhat nicer voice, "Thank you, Mrs. Petrie. I'll take Courtney with me now."

When Aunt Harry and I got back to her apartment, she told me to go into the living room and sit down. She went over to the bar and poured herself a drink. She took a long swallow and then came and sat down opposite me. She looked straight at me and said, not unkindly, "If you've got something to say for yourself, let's hear it now, please."

She watched me so steadily that I felt like I was being hypnotized. I couldn't move my eyes away from hers. "I don't have anything to say for myself, Aunt Harry, because—because I knew I wasn't supposed to ride the subway alone. I'm sorry I did it." I swallowed. "I—I don't have any excuse. I'm sorry if I made you worry."

"*If* you made me worry? *If?* Do you take me for

another Mrs. Van Allen? Do you think I would be dressed and ready to rush off to a party while the child I loved was missing? If you have any doubts, I will tell you I have been worried sick since five o'clock this afternoon."

Her eyes remained fixed on me as I felt my eyes start to fill with tears. She came over and sat down next to me.

"I have just one more thing to say to you before we both forget this dreadful experience." In the most gentle voice I'd ever heard her use, she said, "Thank God you are all right, my pet."

four

WEDNESDAY, August 10. My birthday. During breakfast, Aunt Harry described to me what she had planned for the day. In the afternoon we would go to the Palace Theatre at Broadway and 47th Street, where we would see a musical comedy. Aunt Harry knew how much I loved plays, especially musicals, because my parents and I always see one or two during the week of our annual visit.

After the play we would return to the apartment for my birthday dinner. My parents planned to call early in the evening, and at that time I would open my presents.

"Aunt Harry," I said around a mouthful of bacon and eggs, "would you mind if I invite Courtney to the play and to dinner tonight?"

"Pet, I think that's a splendid idea. After driving home with that poor child last night in her limousine, I think I understand her a little better. She's really quite lonely. Why don't you call her right after breakfast? I'll have my ticket agent reserve another seat right away."

Aunt Harry frowned as I started to devour a piece of toast I had plastered with gobs of butter and jelly. "Pet, please don't inhale your food. It's most unbecoming to a lady, as well as unhealthy."

"Sorry." I reduced gobbling and forced myself to eat more slowly. "I wonder what kind of present I'll get from practically the richest kid in the world?"

Before Aunt Harry could reply, Katie came in and placed an extension phone on the table next to me. "Jan, Courtney Van Allen is on the phone. Would you like to take the call here?"

"Sure." I picked up the receiver as Katie plugged the phone into the wall behind me. "Courtney?"

"Hi, Jan. I have to go downtown with Denise this morning. Do you want to come along?"

"I'll have to ask my Aunt Harry if it's O.K. Where are you going?"

"To visit my shrink."

"Your what?" I asked.

"My shrink," Courtney repeated. "You know, Jan, my psychiatrist."

A psychiatrist! I was shocked! I stared into the receiver and said, "You have a psychiatrist?"

"Of course I have a psychiatrist. His name is

Hugo Malcalm. He's a child psychiatrist. My grandmother says he's the best child psychiatrist in the world."

"Yes, but Courtney, you're not—I mean—are you crazy or something?"

From the other end of the line I heard a long sigh. "Jan, you don't have to be crazy to go to a psychiatrist. My grandmother makes an appointment for me once a week so I can get things out of my system."

"What things?"

"You know, things like frustrations and hostilities."

I didn't exactly understand what Courtney was talking about, so I just said, "Oh."

Courtney could tell I was sort of confused, so she continued to explain. "Jan, everyone has frustrations and hostilities. When I visit Hugo, it helps me get rid of my anxieties."

"Hugo? Do you really call your doctor Hugo?"

"Of course. That's his name, isn't it? Hugo thinks that children and adults should be on a first-name basis. Listen, Jan"—an almost urgent plea crept into her voice—"Jan, I really hope you can go. Hugo's wanted me to bring along a friend for a long time. But you're the only friend I have in New York."

Aunt Harry agreed that I could go with Courtney as long as we made it back in time for the matinee.

When I asked Courtney if she wanted to go to the play with Aunt Harry and me and later to my birthday dinner, she shouted a loud and definite "Yes" into my right eardrum.

"Don't hang up yet, Jan! I'm going to ask Denise to take us shopping after we leave Hugo's because I just thought of what I want to get you for your birthday, but you'll need to come along to make sure we get the right size."

"Really?" I couldn't keep the excitement out of my voice. "What are you getting me?"

"A 'drop dead' shirt and pants exactly like mine."

"Oh." I couldn't keep the disappointment out of my voice, but Courtney didn't seem to notice.

"Don't you think that's neat, Jan?" She didn't wait for an answer. "Then we can both be dropouts."

"But Courtney, I—" I didn't want to hurt her feelings by telling her I hated her beat-up clothes so I just said, "I don't want to drop out."

"Oh." Courtney sounded surprised. After a long pause, she said, "Well, I'll try to think of something else." Courtney told me to meet her in the lobby in thirty minutes.

Aunt Harry thought it was strange that Courtney would want to take me along to visit her analyst, and even stranger to want me to pick out my own birthday present. But by this time Aunt Harry was convinced that Courtney was strange, period.

I took the twenty-three-second elevator down to

the lobby. Courtney wasn't there yet. I walked by a mirror in the lobby and admired the green-and-yellow pants suit I was wearing.

Two security guards were at the desk. "Holy cow, can you believe it?" one of the guards said under his breath. "That Van Allen kid is wearing that same crummy shirt." Both guards stared into the TV monitor as a camera eye followed Courtney and Denise out of the penthouse and down the corridor to the elevator.

Once inside the elevator, they were monitored on a different screen. Denise carried the same large purse she had carried yesterday. I remembered about the gun and wondered if what Courtney had said was true: Did Denise really take a gun along with her everywhere she went? One thing for sure, Denise NEVER smiled. I decided she was a real grouch.

The elevator door opened, and they stepped out. Courtney ran over to me. Denise trailed along behind her.

"Hi, Jan. Are you ready?" Courtney asked.

"What do you mean, is she ready?" Denise wanted to know.

"Jan is going with us," Courtney informed her.

"This is the first I've heard about it," Denise replied rather nastily.

"My grandmother said it was all right if she went with us." There was the ring of a challenge in Courtney's words.

Denise scowled at me. I was beginning to feel very unwanted. "All right," she snapped. "James is waiting, let's go."

James was the chauffeur. He had the Van Allen limousine parked and waiting for us at the curb.

I sank comfortably into the back seat. This was only my second ride in a luxurious limousine, and I leaned back and prepared to enjoy it. It was the longest car I'd ever seen. A window separated the front and back seats. There were two telephones in the back. One was a regular phone. The other was the car phone. It was used by passengers who might need to talk to the chauffeur in the front.

"Denise, I've never talked on a car telephone before. Would you mind if I tried it out?"

"For heaven's sake!" Denise snapped. "What do you mean, 'try it out'? It's a phone. It works like any other phone."

Courtney ignored Denise. She reached for the phone, dialed the operator and handed me the receiver. "Get ready to talk, Jan."

A voice on the other end said, "Hello."

I said, "Hello."

The operator said, "Can I help you?"

I said, "No, thank you. Good-bye." I handed the receiver back to Courtney.

The limousine pulled up in front of a building on Park Avenue. As Denise stepped onto the curb she ordered James to be back in exactly one hour.

When we entered Dr. Malcolm's waiting room,

Denise plopped into the first comfortable chair and started to page through a magazine. I followed wordlessly behind Courtney as she walked up to the receptionist's desk.

"Hi, Annabelle."

The lady behind the desk looked up, her eyes smiling over steel-rimmed glass frames. "Hello, Courtney. You can go in now. Hugo is waiting for you."

"Thanks, Annabelle. I brought a friend along with me today. Her name is Jan Travis."

"I'm so happy you could come with Courtney, Jan," Annabelle said kindly. "Hugo will be delighted to meet you."

Courtney went over to a paneled door engraved with four small gold letters that spelled *hugo*. She knocked once, paused, knocked three times in quick succession, paused, and knocked once more. "It's our secret code," she told me solemnly.

We waited until, from the other side of the door, we heard one knock, a pause, three quick knocks, and a pause followed by a single knock.

The door opened. Behind it stood a tall, skinny man with long, dark hair and a beard streaked with gray. "Courtney!" Dr. Malcalm hopped up and down excitedly. "You have brought a friend!"

Courtney nodded. "Her name is Jan Travis. Jan," she said, turning to me, "this is Hugo."

The doctor hopped up and down again. I leaned

over close to Courtney and whispered, "Do you think he has to go to the bathroom?"

"No," she whispered back, "that's just the way he is. He hops a lot when he talks."

Hugo grabbed my hand and pumped it up and down enthusiastically. "So, Jan, you are a friend of Courtney. Did she tell you how I deal with the tensions of the young mind?"

"She explained a few things to me, Dr. Malcalm."

"No! No! No!" Dr. Malcalm hopped up and down on each no. He abruptly dropped my hand and slapped both his hands on top of his head. He looked horrified. "You must never, NEVER call me by my last name. Call me Hugo, Hugo!"

I stared at the doctor's horror-stricken expression and thought that he must really hate his last name. Or maybe he just loved his first name. I nodded and repeated, "Hugo, Hugo."

"Ah." Hugo's face relaxed. "Yes, that is much better, Jan." He hopped over to the couch. "You see, Jan, the use of the adult's first name by the child is the basis for my therapy." He lay down on the couch. "You do understand?"

"Yes, Hugo, Hugo, I understand." What I really understood was that Hugo was nuts! I whispered to Courtney, "I thought you were the one that's supposed to lie on the couch."

"Hugo says the first one there gets the couch. I forgot to race him for it today."

I looked down at Hugo. He had fallen asleep. "Well, what happens now?" I asked Courtney.

"I think we'll have fun playing Face Baggies in the plastic bubble."

I followed Courtney to the far corner of the room where there was a huge tent that was rounded and covered with clear plastic. Courtney pulled back the flap and led the way inside. Against one wall was a long table covered with paints, crayons, clay, and all kinds of musical instruments. We sat Indian-style on a rug in the center of the plastic bubble while Courtney explained the strange room to me.

"You see, Jan, you're allowed to do anything in here. You can splatter paint all over the place if you want to. Or you can play any instrument that's over there." She motioned toward the table. "You can beat on a drum for a whole hour without anyone telling you to stop—you can even stomp it to pieces if you feel like it.

"Once I played the flute for forty-five minutes while I plastered these walls with clay. I threw blue clay on that wall, yellow clay on that wall, red clay on the wall behind us, and just plain gray clay on the wall to our left. Finally, I mushed all the leftover clay together and stuffed the flute with purple clay."

I stared at her. "What did Dr. Mal—what did Hugo say?"

Courtney shrugged. "Nothing. He was asleep."

Courtney went over to the table, pulled open a

drawer, and took out what looked like plain brown shopping bags.

"Now, you notice, Jan, that the only thing unusual about these bags are the two holes near the top. Those are the eyeholes. Here's what we do: We each take a bag and draw a face on it. It can be an animal face, a monster face, a movie star face—any kind of face. You don't let me see what you're drawing, and I don't let you see what I'm drawing. When we're both finished, I'll call, 'Ready, set, go,' and we pull the bags over our heads, face each other, and carry on a conversation with our new personalities."

I had to admit the Face Baggy game had some possibilities. We spent the entire hour inside the plastic bubble talking with bags over our heads.

Once I was King Kong and Courtney was Wonder Woman. Another time I was a cowboy while Courtney was a mosquito. Then I put on my favorite mask, which was supposed to be Sylvia Sutton, Courtney's mother. Courtney seemed to suddenly lose interest in the game and announced that it was time to stop.

"I think my hour is about over, Jan. We can leave all the masks here. We'd better wake Hugo."

We tiptoed over to the couch and looked down at Hugo, who was snoring loudly. Courtney put a hand on his shoulder and shook him awake. "Hugo, Jan and I are leaving now."

"Huh?" Hugo snapped suddenly to attention and

leaped from the couch. "Oh, yes." He followed us to the door. "Well," he said, hopping first on one foot, then on the other, "I think we have had a very productive session today. Do you not agree?"

"Yes, Hugo," Courtney agreed. "I'll see you next week."

"Good-bye, Jan," Hugo said. "I'm so glad you could come. Getting to know friends of my patients is always helpful."

I nodded politely and said, "Good-bye, Hugo, Hugo."

When we returned to the outer office, we found Denise with her nose buried in a crime magazine. She stood up quickly, tossed the magazine aside, and hoisted the strap of her large purse over her shoulder. "I want to speak to Hugo. I'll meet you two in the limousine in five minutes."

"What do you want to talk to him about?" Courtney was plainly curious.

Denise gave Courtney a cold, hard stare. It was easy to tell she was in her usual rotten mood. "If you must know, Courtney, your grandmother wants me to report back to her about any progress you may have made during today's session with Hugo."

"I can tell her that myself," Courtney said. "I learned how to talk with a paper bag on my head."

"Humph," Denise snorted. "I imagine Hugo will find something more significant than paper bags to report to your grandmother."

"You know, Courtney," I said on our way to the car, "I still don't understand why you don't ask your grandmother to get rid of Denise. She's a terrible governess."

"I told you before, Jan, she's not just a governess. She's really more of a body—"

I interrupted. "She's really more of a bodyguard, right?"

Courtney nodded.

"And that means she is supposed to *guard your body*. But she leaves you alone all the time. Like right now, for instance. Here we are in a deserted hallway waiting for an elevator. If anyone was really serious about kidnapping you, they could do it right now. There's no one around to stop them. There are no people around to witness a crime."

Then Courtney said something that sent a chill down my spine. "There's you," she said quietly.

"Me?" I gulped. "What could I do? I weigh ninety-seven pounds. If I were the only witness, the kidnappers would—"

I felt another chill as Courtney completed my sentence. "You're right," she said. "The kidnappers would have to take you, too."

Just then the double doors of the elevator slid open, and we stepped inside. We were still alone. Our conversation about kidnapping had made the atmosphere eerie.

Courtney was nervous too, even though she

shrugged and said cheerfully, "If I'm ever going to be kidnapped, I think I'd like to have a friend along."

We found James just where we had left him, standing on the curb next to the limousine. He tipped his hat and opened the back door for us.

Denise arrived exactly five minutes later. "Take us home now, James," she ordered.

"Before we go home, Denise, could we stop at Bloomingdale's? I want to buy Jan a birthday present."

"No," Denise replied, her mind made up. "We're going home now. There was a time, Courtney, when I would have trusted you to run into Bloomingdale's by yourself. But after that fiasco you two pulled yesterday, I'm not taking any chances."

Denise looked over at me. I think that was the first time she ever looked directly at me. Our eyes locked together for one brief instant, and I felt myself cringe inside.

"I know that today is your birthday," she said. "But don't worry, you'll get a present from Courtney. All she has to do when she gets home is to pick up the telephone and call Bloomingdale's. I'm sure Mrs. Van Allen has enough pull at Bloomie's to have the package delivered in time for your birthday dinner this evening."

"How did you know about Jan's birthday dinner?" Courtney asked.

"Courtney." Denise shook her head in disgust.

"When will you ever learn that I am your *loving* governess?" In undisguised sarcasm Denise spit out her words. "It's my job to take care of you, *dear*. Although I'm happy to announce that I don't have to accompany you to that stupid play this afternoon. Your grandmother said that Mrs. Petrie will assume that responsibility."

I knew that the play we were going to see had been a big hit on Broadway for months. Thousands of people had seen it, and I had read that it had received nine Tony awards. "Whoever called it a stupid play?" I asked.

Denise gave me another one of her dirty looks. "Why, I said it was stupid. I heard myself say that not ten seconds ago."

"If you haven't seen it," I persisted, "how do you know it's stupid?"

"It's a musical, isn't it? I detest all musicals. They are ridiculous—totally unrealistic."

"What play would you like to see?" I was curious to know.

"*Dracula,*" Denise answered instantly. "It's an excellent play. I've seen it three times since it opened."

I looked over at Courtney, who rolled her eyes with an expression that told me there was no point in trying to have a conversation with Denise.

five

EFORE we left for the theater, Courtney and Aunt Harry had a confrontation that ended in a compromise. Courtney had arrived at our apartment at 1:30 P.M. Since returning home from Hugo's, I had taken a shower, brushed my hair for a full one hundred strokes, changed into my favorite outfit, and eaten lunch. During the same period of time, Courtney had probably eaten lunch. She was still wearing her "drop dead" clothes!

"Courtney," I whispered as I led her into the living room, "Aunt Harry is going to have a fit. I know she'll never take you along if you insist on wearing your 'drop dead' clothes."

"Jan, I've told you a hundred times, I *always* wear these clothes. I have worn them for forty-eight straight days, and I will continue to wear them until certain darn people—"

"Shh! Don't let Aunt Harry hear you. Besides," I said wearily, "I know what you were going to say—'until certain people take the hint and drop dead.' Right?"

Courtney smiled and nodded. "Right."

Aunt Harry was standing by a window looking out over the park when she heard us enter. "Courtney," she said in her most pleasant tone, "you're right on ti—" For one second Aunt Harry's eyes almost popped out of her head, but she regained her composure and said calmly, "Courtney, I guess Jan didn't explain to you that we are going to the *theater*. We are seeing a play on the legitimate New York stage." She spoke very slowly and clearly, the way you would talk to a very young child or to someone who wasn't very bright. "Now, by the way you are dressed, I assume you misunderstood and thought we were going to the roller derby or to a dogfight. But, no, dear—we are going to the *theater*."

Courtney stood with her hands tucked into the hip pockets of her "drop dead" jeans. She had listened politely. "Mrs. Petrie, I know where we are going, but you see, I wear these clothes everywhere. They are a protest symbol. They are a statement, a message that I want to get across to certain people."

Aunt Harry isn't famous for having a great deal of patience. She was struggling to control her temper. "Courtney, I have a message for you. I'm not going to write it on my clothes, I am going to deliver it in plain and simple English." Aunt Harry's words started out low and between clenched teeth, but her voice was rising. "If you want to go with Jan and me this afternoon, you have exactly five minutes to make yourself presentable."

Courtney looked from Aunt Harry to me and back to Aunt Harry. It was easy to see she wasn't very pleased with Aunt Harry's ultimatum.

She stared at Aunt Harry without blinking an eye for a full thirty seconds. Aunt Harry stared right back.

"All right," Courtney said at last, "I'll be back in five minutes."

When she returned, she was wearing a blue-and-pink print blouse and pale blue pants. She looked clean and neat, and there was no message written on any of her clothing. She obviously now met with Aunt Harry's approval. It was later that I discovered that Courtney was still wearing her "drop dead" clothes—*under* the new outfit.

At seven o'clock Aunt Harry, Courtney, and I were seated in Aunt Harry's dining room. We had had a wonderful afternoon. The play turned out to be the best one I'd ever seen. We had just finished one of Katie's delicious meals and were now anxiously awaiting the arrival of my birthday cake. I was especially anxious for Katie to bring the cake because it was then that I'd be allowed to open the presents stacked on the top of the buffet behind me.

The phone rang, and I nearly leaped out of my chair. "Oh, boy! That must be Mom and Dad!"

"Sit down, pet. I'll bring the phone to you."

Once again the phone was plugged in and placed on the table beside me. "Hi, Mom? Dad?" I shouted into the receiver.

"Happy birthday, darling." I heard my mother's good wishes from another continent.

"Hi, Jan." My father was on an extension. "How's everything going?"

"Everything's going great, Dad. Aunt Harry, Courtney, and I have just finished dinner, and I'm about to open my presents."

"Courtney Van Allen? Is she there, too?" asked my mother.

"Yes," I replied. "And Mom, she's not—" I looked at Courtney, who was listening to my every word.

My mother must have realized I couldn't finish what I had been going to say because she finished it for me. "You mean she's not crazy." She laughed.

"Well," I said, still looking at Courtney, "maybe a little, but she's really neat, Mom."

"Honey, this is a long-distance call," my dad said. "So how about opening our present?"

I didn't have to be asked twice. Aunt Harry had placed the present on the table in front of me. I don't like to be delicate, like some girls when they unwrap gifts. Once I went to a wedding shower with my mother, and it took the bride-to-be at least five minutes to unwrap each package. First she'd remove the bow and say, "What a pretty bow!" Then she'd slip off the ribbon as carefully as a surgeon performing an operation. Next, she'd delicately tuck a finger under the tape at one end of the box and slowly pull it away from the paper as if the world would end if any damage came to the wrapping paper. Well, that bride-to-be didn't know much about opening presents, but I do. And, since this was a long-distance call, there was no time to waste.

I reached for my parents' gift, snatched off the bow, popped the ribbon, and tore away the paper— all in three seconds flat. Inside the box, all protected with Styrofoam, was a portable TV, AM-FM radio, and cassette tape recorder.

"Mom, Dad," I said happily into the receiver. "It's beautiful! I love it! Thank you!"

"You're welcome, baby," my dad said.

"We're glad you like it, Jan," my mother said. "I guess we'd better hang up now, darling. We both miss you very much."

"We'll call again in a few days," my dad promised. "Have a happy birthday and take care of yourself, O.K.?"

After the three of us finished with our good-byes, my parents asked to speak with Aunt Harry. It was seven-thirty when my parents hung up.

"Take care of yourself," my father had said. I

think it's a good thing we can't see into the future because that evening was one of the nicest times I've ever had. I could never have imagined what was going to happen to Courtney and me within the next two hours.

Katie came in carrying my birthday cake. She placed it, with all twelve candles blazing away, in front of me. That seemed to be the signal for everyone to start singing "Happy Birthday." When they had finished, I managed to blow out all the candles in a single breath. Katie served the cake and then, at Aunt Harry's request, joined us at the table.

"My pet," Aunt Harry exclaimed, "I have three presents for you. Which one would you like to open first?"

I selected the smallest one first. It was a wallet with the initials of a famous Italian store forming a pattern in the wine-colored leather. Inside was a thousand-dollar bill! I was speechless. I looked at Aunt Harry and then unfolded the bill and checked again to see if I had counted the correct amount of zeros. "One thousand dollars!" I choked.

"It's for your college education fund, pet," Aunt Harry informed me.

I got up and hugged her. "Thanks, Aunt Harry."

I opened the largest present next. For the first time, I noticed that small holes had been poked into the sides of what was an enormous box. I quickly unpeeled the wrapping.

As I was about to remove the top of the box, Aunt Harry warned, "Gently, now, pet, very gently. I don't want you to frighten Calvin."

"Calvin?" Courtney and I said in unison.

I peeked cautiously inside. All ten feet of a large boa constrictor were curled into a tight ball. I must have disturbed Calvin's nap because he suddenly lifted his head and angrily flicked a black-forked tongue in my direction.

"Merciful heavens!" gasped Katie, dropping her fork with a bang onto Aunt Harry's fine china.

Courtney's eyes nearly popped out of her head. Her mouth hung open in astonishment, even though it was full of birthday cake.

I didn't think it would be polite of me to tell Aunt Harry that I was terrified of my birthday present, so I said nothing but flattened myself against the back of my chair.

Aunt Harry was obviously delighted in her choice of gifts for me. She reached into the box and petted Calvin. "There, there, sweetheart. I'm afraid we're frightening him. Come on, little Cal." She spoke soothingly and lovingly to my birthday present. She wrapped her hands around Calvin, lifted him out of the box, and draped him over her shoulders.

"Mrs. Petrie," Courtney gulped, nearly choking, "don't put that snake around your neck. A boa constrictor can crush you to death!"

"Nonsense, my dear," Aunt Harry said, totally

unconcerned. "Calvin has been a household pet on the South American plantation where I order my Barkletts."

"Your what?" asked Courtney.

"Never mind, Courtney. I'll explain later. Really, Aunt Harry, what am I going to do with a boa constrictor?"

"Actually, pet," Aunt Harry replied, "I'm donating him to the Bronx Zoo in your name. Such a donation will make you a lifetime member of the New York Zoological Society. As a member of that illustrious group you are entitled to many benefits. You'll be given a lifetime pass to any zoo in the state, and you will receive a free copy of *Animal Lover* magazine every month."

"Oh." A free pass and a free magazine sounded a lot better to me than a free snake. "Well, that will be very nice, Aunt Harry. Thank you."

"You're quite welcome, pet." Aunt Harry removed Calvin from around her neck and helped him coil himself around the leg of the buffet. "And now, Jan," she said, returning to her seat at the table, "it's time for your third present."

I handled Aunt Harry's third present more cautiously than the box Calvin had arrived in—just in case she planned a double lifetime membership in the New York Zoological Society.

Aunt Harry's last gift turned out to be a red leather five-year diary with my initials embossed on the cover in gold. When Katie saw the diary, she breathed a sigh of relief.

"O.K., Jan. It's time for my present now," said Courtney eagerly.

Packed inside a fancy box were three cassette tapes. "Hey, Courtney, just what I need." I was referring to my new tape recorder. "How did you know?"

"I was going to get you a gold disco shirt from Bloomingdale's, but your aunt suggested buying some tapes." Courtney smiled, pleased to see that I was happy with her present.

"Yes," said Aunt Harry. "I told Courtney that I knew you'd enjoy some Beethoven."

"Well," Courtney hesitated, "they aren't exactly Beethoven, Mrs. Petrie. I bought Jan tapes of my favorite group—The Blue Moo-Moos."

"The Blue—" Aunt Harry couldn't bring herself to finish the sentence.

"Yeah, they're really neat, Mrs. Petrie. You see," Courtney continued enthusiastically, "there are five members in this rock group. They wear jeans and blue cowhide vests, and right in the middle of every song, the drummer tosses his sticks in the air and moos two times. He always moos exactly two times. No more, no less. You're going to love them, Jan."

I smiled at the expression on Aunt Harry's face. For once, she was actually speechless. "Thanks, Courtney." I didn't know if I'd like the Blue

Moo-Moos or not, but I was sure I'd rather have them than a "drop dead" outfit.

"Jan, I have one more surprise for you," Courtney said happily. "You're going to come up with me to my grandmother's penthouse and spend the night."

I looked at Aunt Harry. "That's right, pet," she confirmed. "I've already talked to Mrs. Van Allen, and she's expecting you."

"Great! I'll take my new recorder and Blue Moo-Moo tapes with me."

"Thank God," sighed Aunt Harry. "That is," she stammered, not wanting to hurt Courtney's feelings, "I mean, that's a fine idea, pet."

By nine o'clock Courtney wound up owing me two thousand three hundred and forty-five Monopoly dollars. We had just finished listening to the last of the Blue Moo-Moo tapes when Courtney declared me the official Monopoly champion.

Courtney then declared it was time to change into our pajamas and settle down to an evening of TV. When she unbuttoned her theater blouse, she puffed out her chest and revealed her "drop dead" T-shirt. She noticed me staring.

"Your aunt sure doesn't understand much about protesting," she said as she stepped out of her blue theater pants to reveal her "drop dead" pants underneath.

We started fooling around with my miniature TV set. The screen was exactly three inches square in size. After a while, Courtney suggested that we should stop straining our eyes and watch her TV set instead.

"What would you like to watch, Jan?"

"I don't know. What's on?"

"What's on? Are you serious?" Courtney asked in surprise. "We don't have to watch what's on. This is a videotape recorder, Jan. I have a library of over two hundred tapes. Name any movie. Go on," she dared me, "I'll probably have a copy of it. I've got every good movie ever made. One thing I can say about my film library is this: I don't keep tapes of *boring* movies, only the good ones. Name any monster movie ever made. What about this one?" She pulled a tape from the shelf in front of me. *"King Kong Eats Chinatown."*

"Well, O.K." I tossed several large pillows on the floor in front of the TV, plopped down in the middle of them, and made myself comfortable.

King Kong had eaten only two small boats and one medium-sized bridge when Denise interrupted his menu with a knock on the door. She didn't wait to be invited in. "Courtney, get dressed," she ordered. "We're leaving for—" She broke off in mid-sentence and scowled at me. "What are *you* doing here?"

I had never before met an adult as rude as

Denise. I felt hurt because I could see she didn't want me around and angry because I didn't think I deserved to be treated so impolitely.

Courtney took over. "Denise, I've already talked to Grandma. She's happy that Jan's staying overnight with me."

"Overnight!" Denise seemed shocked and confused. "Er—I'll be right back," she said, leaving as abruptly as she had entered.

Courtney shrugged and we turned our attention back to King Kong.

Denise returned five minutes later. This time she didn't even bother to knock. "Girls, get dressed immediately. We're leaving for Long Island."

"What?" asked Courtney in surprise. "Now? In the middle of the night?"

"It's hardly the middle of the night," Denise corrected her. "If we leave now, we should be there by midnight."

"I don't understand," Courtney protested. "Why are we going to Long Island?"

"Mrs. Van Allen is expecting houseguests to arrive from Europe tomorrow. She wants to entertain them on Long Island instead of here in the city."

Courtney got up and snapped off King Kong just as he was starting to pound on his chest and stamp out a platoon of marines. "Jan, I'll talk to my grandmother and—"

"No!" Denise interrupted emphatically. "I mean

—er—your grandmother just left for a party. She's planning to drive out later."

"Well, what about Jan? Can she come too?"

"Yes. Mrs. Van Allen is expecting me to drive you both out to Long Island."

I stood up and pulled my overnight bag out from under the bed. "All right, but I'd better call Aunt Harry first."

"There's no need," Denise protested. "I've just called Mrs. Petrie. She asked me to tell you to have a good time."

Courtney and I followed Denise out the front lobby of the Fifth Avenue Central Park Tower. We waited silently for James to pull the limousine up to the curb.

But it wasn't James or the Van Allen limousine that arrived for us. The car was a silver Courtney. Denise opened the back door and practically shoved us inside. She jumped into the front seat and we were halfway down the block before I realized who was driving the Courtney.

"Hugo!" Courtney gasped. "What—?"

"Good evening, young ladies." Hugo beamed, bouncing up and down blissfully behind the steering wheel.

"Denise said we were going to my grandmother's house on Long Island," Courtney said in a puzzled voice. "I don't understand, Hugo. Are you coming with us?"

Denise's profile was silhouetted in the darkness of the car as she half turned and spoke to us over her shoulder. "No, Courtney. I didn't say we were going to your grandmother's house. What I said was that we were going to Long Island."

"Actually, young ladies," Hugo explained, "we are going to visit *my* grandmother."

Courtney and I looked at each other. I knew that she was as confused as I was.

"*You* have a grandmother?" Courtney blurted out in obvious amazement.

Hugo seemed amused. "Of course. Miss Fannie Violet. A charming lady. She celebrated her ninety-eighth birthday last week. But she's as spry as an eighty-eight-year-old.

"Granny, or Miss Fannie, as I sometimes call her, was a world-famous star of the stage and screen." Hugo was getting so carried away telling Courtney and me about his grandmother that I noticed he wasn't keeping his eyes on the traffic ahead of us. He continued to speak in the general direction of the back seat. "Old Granny was a real beauty. She was one of the biggest stars of the silent screen. She even made a picture with Rudolph Valen—"

"Hugo!" Denise's scream pierced my eardrums.

Hugo applied all his weight onto the brake pedal. The Courtney screeched to a halt, missing the car in front of us by a millimeter.

"Crazy New York drivers!" Hugo shouted.

"Hugo, I don't understand why you're taking Jan

and me to visit your grandmother," Courtney said.

"As I told you, Courtney," Hugo replied, "Miss Fannie is a charming lady." Forgetting our near brush with death, he turned and smiled into the back seat. "I know you will both enjoy meeting her. I am sure that Mrs. Van Allen realizes what a treat it will be, not only for you young ladies to meet Miss Fannie but for her guests as well. Your grandmother and her friends will be joining us in a day or two."

"But, Denise, you told us that Grandma would be driving out later tonight."

"No, Courtney." Denise sighed impatiently. "I do wish you'd listen. I simply said she'd be coming out later. Mrs. Van Allen thought you girls might enjoy going to Miss Fannie's home for a therapeutic meditation session."

"A what?" Courtney demanded.

Hugo again turned his attention away from the road. "As your psychiatrist, Courtney, I believe that such a session will be highly beneficial to your emotional development."

"Excuse me, Dr. Mal—er—Hugo," I said, trying not to sound as nervous as I felt. "Maybe I should go back to my aunt's. I don't think I need to go to this meditation session."

"Nonsense!" Hugo declared. "Everyone needs to meditate. You are very fortunate because there will be just the two of you attending this session. And myself of course." He smiled proudly. "I will be the leader."

"I'm surprised Aunt Harry didn't talk to me about this first."

"What difference does it make?" Denise nearly snapped my head off. "We're on our way to Miss Fannie's, and that's that!" After a moment she leaned her head back against the car seat and said in a dreamy sigh, "Miss Fannie's place is peaceful and quiet and lovely. You'll both have a wonderful time, I'm sure."

"You've been to Miss Fannie's house before?" Courtney didn't try to hide her curiosity.

Hugo bobbed up and down. "Yes, she has. As a matter of fact, Courtney, Denise and I have known one another for several years."

"Well, that's certainly news to me," Courtney announced. "How come you never told me you knew each other?"

"Courtney, some things are just none of your business!" Denise informed her.

Hugo reached over to pat Denise's hand. "My sweet one," he said, gently reprimanding her, "remember I am a child psychiatrist. An adult should never speak to a child in such a manner. What Denise is trying to say, Courtney, is that some things are just none of your business."

"Denise, you mean"—Courtney stammered in shock—"Hugo is your boyfriend?"

Hugo giggled. "That is correct, Courtney. And Denise," he said, still patting her hand, "is my sweet one!"

Courtney and I stared at each other, unable to believe our ears. What a pair! I was beginning to think they deserved each other.

At eleven-thirty Hugo pulled the Courtney off the main highway and drove for a mile along a dirt road that led to a remote beach. He parked the car near a pier. The only thing we could see in the darkness was the outline of the pier, a small speedboat, and the blackness of the ocean.

"Where are we?" I asked nervously.

"We are on the eastern tip of Long Island," explained Hugo. "Miss Fannie lives on a small island about three miles due south."

"The only access to Miss Fannie's home is by boat," Denise added.

"Unless you are a bird." Hugo laughed at his corny joke.

We followed behind Hugo and Denise as they led us onto the pier. One by one we climbed down a wooden ladder and hopped into the speedboat.

My mother always told me I had an overactive imagination from reading too many mystery novels. Well, it was sure active now. From somewhere deep inside me, I started to tremble. I tried to tell myself it was because of the chilly ocean breeze, but I knew that wasn't the reason. Here I was with the richest kid in the world, her grouchy governess, and a weird psychiatrist. I swallowed hard and concentrated on controlling my trembling body.

The four of us arranged our luggage in the boat. Waves lapped against its fiberglass sides as Hugo fished in his pockets for the key to start the engine.

"Hugo, how do you know where you're going?" Courtney was afraid, too. I had never heard such a high pitch in her voice before.

"Hugo knows what he's doing," Denise said confidently.

"Of course I do. It is very simple. I start the boat and aim it in the direction of Miss Fannie's island."

"It's pitch black out here." Courtney's voice rose a notch as she repeated, "How can you tell where you're going?"

"For crying out loud, Courtney!" Denise was disgusted by all our questions. "Haven't you ever heard of a compass?"

"Oh," Courtney replied in a small voice.

For the next ten minutes we bounced over choppy waves. By the time we reached the island, we were drenched in cold ocean spray.

Hugo slowed the boat as we approached a long white pier. He carefully maneuvered the boat into a slip next to an enormous yacht. In the darkness I was just able to make out the name of the larger yacht: *Miss Fannie*.

Wordlessly, Hugo switched off the motor and

tossed an anchor chain around a docking post. One by one we followed Hugo up a ladder, Courtney and I awkwardly trying to climb while juggling our luggage.

Once we were on the pier, Hugo wasted no time. He grabbed Denise's hand, and the two of them hopped happily down the white steps of the dock, across the short expanse of sandy beach, and along a narrow gravel path lined with carefully manicured hedges. Courtney and I struggled to keep up with them.

In the darkness it was impossible to get a clear view of the area. When the gravel path came to an end, we followed Hugo over about an acre of green lawn. I was able to make out the silhouette of a Victorian mansion. The house was dark except for one small window on the ground floor.

When we reached the house, Hugo crept through shrubbery until he stood in front of the lighted window. We all tiptoed quietly behind him.

He tapped lightly four times, then, leaning as close to the window as possible, he whispered, "It is Junior."

From inside came a thin, crackling voice, "Junior?"

Exasperated, Courtney threw her suitcase down on the ground and screamed, "Junior!"

"Courtney! Will you shut up!" demanded Denise, recovering from shock.

Hugo tried to calm Denise. "Now, my sweet one.

That is no way to speak to a child. Courtney," he said gently, "what Denise means is that she wants you to button your lip. Come, follow me. Miss Fannie will be ringing for William. He should be unlocking the door at any moment."

We walked to the front of the house and waited on a flagstone porch that held all varieties of potted trees and plants. There were beveled glass windows on either side of the massive double doors. A light shone from inside, and through the windows we could see a shadowy form approaching.

The door opened. A man about a hundred years old, with white lizard skin and hair like cotton, bowed to greet Hugo. "Good evening, Sir Junior." His voice was as shaky as his body.

"William." Hugo returned the bow. "You're looking well," he lied. "I have brought two young guests. They will be staying here for the next few days. Of course, you remember Denise? And"—he gestured toward Courtney and me—"this is Courtney and her friend. What is your name again, young lady?"

"Jan," I told him.

"Yes, that is correct. This is Jan," he explained to William.

Hugo hopped up and down excitedly and opened his arms wide as shuffling footsteps approached the entrance hall. Hugo's grandmother, with the aid of a cane, hobbled into Hugo's waiting arms.

"Granny! Miss Fannie!" he said, embracing her.

She let him kiss both of her withered old cheeks before she lifted her cane and brought it down hard on Hugo's big toe. "Junior, you told me you'd be bringing two children, but you never told me about her." She pointed a bent white finger at Denise.

Denise looked uncomfortable and turned a deep shade of red. I couldn't tell if she was embarrassed or just plain mad.

"Miss Fannie, you know that Denise is my sweetheart," Hugo explained.

During this conversation I was trying my best not to stare at Miss Fannie's hair. It was purple!

I glanced at Courtney, who managed to pull her eyes away from Miss Fannie long enough to whisper, "She's got purple hair!"

"Oh, all right!" Miss Fannie glared at Denise and banged her cane down on the hardwood floor. "Since you're here, you might as well stay in the same room you had before. Junior," she shook her head sadly at Hugo, "you never did have any sense about women."

Miss Fannie hobbled over to Courtney and me. Because she was bent with age, she wasn't much taller than we were. She peered at us through thick steel-rimmed glasses. Placing both hands on top of her cane, she swayed forward. "Children, you're both welcome as long as you remember what the Bible says: 'Children should be seen, not heard.'"

"Miss Fannie," Hugo interrupted. "I don't think the Bible says—"

Miss Fannie banged her cane to silence Hugo. "If it doesn't, it should," she said, firmly closing the subject. Turning back to us, she said, "Now then, children, William will show you to your room. Junior, I want to speak to you alone. You will come to my room for a few minutes before you retire," she ordered.

"Old biddy," Denise whispered under her breath.

"I beg your pardon, miss?" William was obviously a little hard of hearing.

"Oh, nothing, William." Denise raised her voice and shouted, "I know where my room is, I'll find it myself." She picked up her bag and started up the stairs. Without a backward glance she said, "I'll see you two in the morning."

"Young ladies, follow me," William said as he headed for the grand staircase.

At the foot of the staircase was a chair that seemed to be attached to the side of the wall. I was about to ask Courtney what the chair was for when William reached the bottom stair and turned his ancient body slowly around to face us. He then carefully lowered his old bones into the chair. He pushed a button on the wall and the chair glided backward up the stairs. A chair escalator!

Courtney and I, carrying our suitcases, followed along behind William and the chair until it reached the first landing.

"Young ladies," William panted as if the ride had

worn him out, "your room is on the third floor." He panted again and slowly raised a wrinkled hand to point the way up to a second staircase. As we started in the direction he indicated, he said, "Breakfast is always served exactly at eight-thirty. Please be on time." He paused to catch his breath. "Miss Fannie cannot tolerate tardiness."

We nodded and watched William push a button and descend to the ground floor. Then we climbed the narrow spiral steps that led to the third floor.

"There must be only one room up here," Courtney said, stopping in front of the door at the top of the stairs. She opened the door and snapped on a light.

We carried our suitcases to the center of the room, where we stood speechless while our eyes traveled over what once must have been the most splendid playroom in the world.

The corners of the room seemed to be four separate rooms in themselves. The southeast corner housed a collection of trains mounted on a three-level platform that contained miniature cities, parks, farms, and countrysides, each with their own miniature people, cars, buildings, animals, telephone poles, and streetlights. A ladder was attached to the platform. Built into the wall, beside the ladder, was a complicated-looking control panel to operate the entire fantasy world.

"Wow!" Even Courtney was in awe.

Together we investigated the southwest corner.

It was a small but functional laboratory. It contained powders, bottles, and vials of every color, size, shape, and description.

"Wow!" Courtney repeated. "I'll bet when Hugo was a boy he wanted to grow up to be a doctor."

"Or a mad scientist." An image of Frankenstein shot through my mind, and I shuddered.

We walked to the opposite end of the room. This section of the giant bedroom-playroom was actually a library. Floor-to-ceiling shelves, crammed full of books, lined the walls. A globe resting in a wooden floorstand, a desk, filing cabinets, and a typewriter made the library complete.

The last corner was a sitting room with a couch, two chairs, an assortment of tables and lamps, and a radio in an old-fashioned cabinet that must have come from the 1940s.

We returned to the center of the room. I placed my overnight bag on the king-sized bed. Courtney left her suitcase where she had first tossed it, in the middle of the floor. She stood silently gazing about. I knew that she was as impressed by Hugo's old room as much as I was. But it soon became evident that she wasn't just admiring the room. She was looking for something in particular.

I sat down on the edge of the bed and started to remove my shoes. "What are you looking for, Courtney?"

Her eyes continued to move about as a frown appeared across her forehead. "Doesn't it seem weird to you, Jan, that this room has almost everything except a telephone?"

I had to admit it did seem sort of strange. "Wait!" A thought had suddenly occurred to me. "I bet there's a phone in here." I opened the door that led to the adjoining bathroom. I smiled at my discovery. "Come look at this, Courtney." Built into the wall, just beside the toilet-paper fixture, was a blue telephone that exactly matched the blue tiles of the sink and floor.

"O.K." Courtney seemed relieved. The toilet lid was down. Courtney sat on top of it, picked up the receiver, and started to dial.

"Courtney, it's one-thirty in the morning. Who are you calling?"

"My grandmother. There's something weird about her not saying anything to me about coming out here with Hugo."

I nodded. "I know. I'm surprised Aunt Harry didn't talk to me first, too."

Courtney frowned into the receiver and returned it to its wall cradle. Her voice sounded strangely hoarse. "Jan, there's no dial tone. It's out of order."

We returned to the bedroom and wordlessly started changing into our pajamas. Now that we had expressed our fears, there was a new tension in the room. Neither of us understood it, but both of us felt it.

Just before turning out the lights, Courtney said, "We'll just have to use one of the downstairs phones. I promise, Jan, first thing in the morning I'll call my grandmother and ask her to get us off this island. If she wants to know why, I'll tell her it stinks."

As it turned out, that was a promise Courtney wasn't able to keep.

six

AT six o'clock the next morning I opened my eyes and was instantly wide awake. This was unusual for me because I'm a night person. It takes me a long time to get going in the morning, and I almost always feel my most alert during the evening hours.

That first morning at Hugo's was different, though. I didn't go through my normal routine of lazy stretches and moans and burrowing my head deep into my pillow to drift off into a pleasant semiconscious state. Instead, I lay on my back and surveyed the room as I gave a great deal of thought to my present situation. I had privately felt there was something strange about Hugo and Denise from the first moment I had met them.

I turned toward Courtney, who was still sleeping, rolled into a tight ball on her side of the bed. I hoped she wouldn't sleep too late. The sooner she called her grandmother to come get us, the happier I would be.

In the light of day, Hugo's boyhood room seemed even more magnificent than it had the night before. There were windows on three sides of the room. I sat in one of the overstuffed chairs and looked out across a beautiful green lawn that stretched all the way to the shore. For a long time I sat there, looking out across what I knew had to be one of the finest estates in America.

I could hear the waves breaking on the beach, and I felt myself start to relax. Even if Hugo, Denise, and the old lady with the purple hair were a little strange, why should I be afraid? It might even be fun to spend a few days on the island. With this thought in mind, I went to the closet where I had put my overnight bag. I took out a comb, a toothbrush, toothpaste, and some fresh clothing and went into the bathroom to shower.

Twenty minutes later, I returned to the chair in the sitting-room area and waited for Courtney to wake up. About half an hour passed.

One thing about Courtney: When she wakes up, she doesn't waste any time. "Jan! Why didn't you wake me up? I told you I wanted to call my grandmother first thing in the morning."

"This is the first thing in the morning," I explained.

Courtney didn't answer that remark. She was too

busy searching the floor for her clothes. "Jan, will you help me look?" she asked impatiently. "I can't find my left tennis shoe and my 'drop dead' shirt. Oh, never mind. Here they are." She got down on her hands and knees and crawled under the bed. On her way to the bathroom she shook sand out of her shoes.

The bathroom door opened a few minutes later. "Jan, can I borrow some toothpaste? I forgot to bring some. I forgot a toothbrush, too, but I'll just squeeze some toothpaste onto a washcloth and wash my teeth."

Five minutes later, the bathroom door opened again. "O.K.," Courtney said, filled with determination. "Let's go find a telephone." She opened the bedroom door and paused on the top step. She lowered her voice. "Don't make any noise," she told me. "Just keep your fingers crossed that everyone's still sleeping. That way we won't have to put up with any arguments about me calling my grandmother."

All the doors on the second floor were closed, so we silently made our way down the main staircase to the entryway. There was no phone in the entrance hall, but that wasn't too surprising. We went into the living room. Again, no phone. I followed Courtney across the hall into the library. No phone. We retraced our steps from the library through the hallway into the living room. We looked at each other and at the same time headed to the dining room. No phone. We pushed through a swinging door into an enormous old kitchen. No phone.

We retraced our steps back to the entry hall and found a hallway that led to the west wing of the house. The first door we came to on the right-hand side of the corridor was closed. Without any hesitation, Courtney turned the doorknob and started to enter the room.

"Courtney," I whispered in alarm. "I don't think we should go in. This is probably Miss Fannie's room!"

The warning came too late. I followed Courtney's gaze to where Miss Fannie lay in an enormous four-poster bed. I gasped and clamped a hand over my mouth. Miss Fannie's purple hair was hanging over one of the posters at the foot of her bed!

Courtney drew a quick breath, and I could tell she was struggling not to scream. "Jan, Look!"

My gaze moved from the purple wig to Hugo's old grandma, who slept propped up on two king-sized pillows. Except for a few wisps of white hair on the very top of her head, Miss Fannie was totally bald!

Courtney and I both jumped as Miss Fannie breathed deeply, snorted once, and then slept on in a gentle but continuous snore. We backed out of the room.

When we reached the double doors at the end of the hall, Courtney paused and with uncustomary caution slowly tiptoed into the room. I tiptoed in behind her. We found ourselves in the middle of a movie theater! The theater held four rows, each row with eight identical chairs. Each chair was actually a reclining rocker covered in fine purple leather. A total of thirty-two chairs faced a giant-sized movie screen.

For a long time neither of us spoke. Then we became aware of the framed posters that hung like great works of art along the theater walls. We soon realized that every poster, from floor to ceiling, was an advertisement for a silent movie starring Fannie Violet. In one, titled *The Vampire's Coffin*, Fannie Violet smiled, radiantly unaware that behind her stood a black-caped man with two long fangs about to bite her in the neck.

Another poster showed a cowboy leaning out of his saddle, his face buried in Fannie Violet's purple hair. I guess the cowboy was supposed to be kissing Miss Fannie's hair, but instead it looked as if he were trying to eat it.

"Look at this one, Courtney," I said, pointing to a poster called *Pamela and the Palomino.* The picture showed Fannie Violet tied to a railroad track and screaming bloody murder because a speeding freight train was almost on top of her. Chewing at the ropes that bound her wrists was a blond horse. I didn't have to see the movie to know that the palomino would save Pamela in the nick of time.

In the dozens of pictures that covered the wall,

whether she was laughing or crying or screaming hysterically or just wistfully staring into the eyes of a handsome co-star, one fact remained the same: about seventy years ago, Miss Fannie had been beautiful.

"I know one thing," Courtney declared, staring at the youthful Fannie Violet, "I never want to be old."

"There's not much choice, Courtney. Everyone gets older sooner or later."

"Not me!" Courtney sounded very determined. "What I'm going to do when I'm about forty is start to eat lots of yogurt and move to a cold climate—Alaska or Norway. Freezing slows down the aging process."

I was going to tell her that I had seen plenty of pictures of old Eskimos when something else drew Courtney's attention. The opposite wall was covered with more posters, which both of us had assumed were about Fannie Violet's silent film career. As we looked closer, I noticed that these posters were much more up to date. It was Courtney who realized their real significance.

"It's my mother!"

She was right. Every poster, every picture, was of Sylvia Sutton. The whole span of her twenty-year career was chronicled on this wall: from teen-age movie idol to present-day TV star. We silently surveyed each picture.

"Your mother is really beautiful, Courtney."

When there was no reply, I said, "Don't you think so?"

Courtney's eyes lingered a moment longer on her mother before she turned and said abruptly, "No! I told you before, Jan, my mother stinks!"

"How come you don't like your own mother, Courtney?"

Courtney glared at me. "That's none of your business," she snapped. "Come on, let's get out of here." She started to march out of the room.

I knew that I had upset her, and I was about to apologize when I spotted a phone on a table next to one of the chairs. "Wait, Courtney! Here's what we've been looking for all morning: a phone!"

"Where?"

"Oh." On closer inspection I saw that the phone had no dial. It was just an extension phone.

"Well," Courtney said, "this phone has to be connected to another phone. All we have to do is find it."

There was a projection booth in the back of the room. The door was open. Courtney snapped on a light and immediately found the second phone. She eagerly lifted the receiver to her ear. I knew from her letdown expression that it was out of order.

"There's no dial tone." Courtney replaced the receiver and for a moment looked so frustrated that I was afraid she might start to cry.

"Don't worry, Courtney," I said, trying to sound more confident than I felt. "This is a big house.

There has to be a telephone someplace."

While Courtney wore a depressed look and stared at the floor, I looked around the small projection booth. It was lined with shelves containing hundreds of cans of film. Each can had the title of a movie printed on it. As far as I could tell, every movie ever made by Fannie Violet and Sylvia Sutton had to be right here in this room.

Courtney became interested in the movie titles. "Jan, I can understand why Miss Fannie has all her old movies, but why would she collect my mother's films?"

We had left the theater and had started back to the main section of the house. "I don't know, Courtney. Maybe Miss Fannie is your mother's number-one fan."

We entered the entrance hall. It appeared that no one else was up yet, so we walked to the library and went outside through French doors of stained glass. We walked across a flagstone terrace and down two steps that led to a wide lawn on the south side of the house. From inside we heard a grandfather clock chime eight times. We still had half an hour until breakfast time.

"You know," I said, still thinking about the Sylvia Sutton posters and films, "maybe Hugo has a crush on your mother."

Courtney made no comment.

"Or," I continued, "maybe that collection of your mother's films belongs to old William."

Courtney giggled at that, but became immediately serious again. "There's something weird about all this, Jan. I mean, we couldn't find a single phone that works in the whole house. You have to admit that's weird. And the weirdest thing of all is that my grandmother and your aunt never said anything at all to us about our coming out to this island with Hugo."

"I'm worried too," I admitted, but trying to look on the bright side, I said, "As long as we have to be stranded on an island, there's no other island in the world I'd rather be on than this one. It's got everything."

"Yeah, everything but a phone," Courtney said gloomily.

"Look!" I pointed to the far end of the lawn. "A croquet set!" All nine wickets were firmly placed in the ground, ready for a game. We found a single weather-beaten mallet near one wicket.

Courtney, who didn't care to look on the bright side of things, was growing angrier and more frustrated by the second at not being able to call her grandmother. She kicked the mallet with her tennis shoe. "This place stinks! I've had it, Jan!" she declared. "We just have to go in and DEMAND that they take us back to New York City today." She angrily kicked the mallet a second time. "We have to let them know we won't take no for an answer."

I sighed. "What do you mean? What can we do if they refuse to take us back?"

Courtney carefully considered my question. "I might have to throw a fit."

"A fit?"

"You know, Jan. A temper tantrum. Of course, I haven't had to throw a real temper tantrum for years, but I know I can still do it."

"What kind of temper tantrum are you talking about, Courtney?"

"Come on, Jan." She sounded annoyed. "Don't tell me you haven't ever had a temper tantrum."

"Well," I said, trying to remember, "once when I was about five years old I got furious with my mother because the ice cream truck was driving by and she said I couldn't have any."

"What did you do?"

"I cried and tossed a vase on the floor."

Courtney nodded in approval. "Good. Did you get the ice cream?"

"No, I got a spanking," I answered.

"Oh." Courtney seemed disappointed in me. "That only shows that you don't know anything about temper tantrums. Once I got rid of three governesses in a single month," she said proudly.

"Courtney." I shook my head. "There has got to be a better way."

"Maybe you're right," she agreed, kicking the mallet a third time, harder than before. "If they refuse to take us back today, I'm going to tear Miss Fannie's house apart piece by piece." She punctuated this threat by bending over and picking up the croquet mallet. She looked like Bionic Woman Junior as she placed the mallet over her knee and cracked it in two. Courtney smiled, pleased with her performance. Tossing the remains of the mallet over her shoulder, she marched across the lawn and toward the back of the mansion. There was a look of determination on her face. "Follow me," she bravely ordered.

She marched down a corridor and into the kitchen and was about to march into the dining room when the door, swinging open from the opposite side, plastered her against the wall.

Hugo bounced in. "Ah, good morning, young lady," he said to me. Pulling back the door, he spotted Courtney trying her best not to pass out after the knock on the head she'd just received. "Courtney, come out from behind the door. It is much too early for hide-and-seek. We can play that game later."

"Hugo," Courtney sputtered, rubbing the knot that was forming on the top of her head. "I'm not playing hide-and-seek."

"Good for you, my young friend." Hugo was pleased. "I am glad you have decided to wait until later to play that game." He hopped over to the refrigerator.

"Hugo, Jan and I want to go back to the city today," she said in a voice that was not quite as demanding as she had intended it to be.

"Ah, young ladies." Hugo appeared not to have

heard Courtney's demand. He poked his head into the refrigerator. "You are in for a splendid treat," he said, placing a bowl of eggs and a carton of milk on the kitchen counter. "An omelet à la Hugo."

"Hugo," Courtney repeated, "Jan and I want to go back to New York City today."

Hugo again seemed not to hear Courtney. He spoke to me. "You have no doubt tasted spinach omelet?"

I nodded.

"Well," he continued, picking up an egg, "my specialty is cauliflower omelet à la Hugo."

Courtney was not used to being ignored. She jammed her small body between Hugo and the kitchen counter. Her face turned purple and her eyes bulged as she screeched into Hugo's face, "HUGO! JAN AND I WANT TO GO BACK TO NEW YORK CITY TODAY!"

Courtney's words must have pierced Hugo's eardrums. He nearly dropped the egg he was holding, but he managed to reply calmly, "Surely you do not wish to leave Miss Fannie's island paradise so soon? Can it be possible that you do not care for my old granny, Miss Fannie?" Hugo wore such a hurt expression that I thought he might burst into tears.

Courtney must have thought so too because she lowered her voice and said politely, "Well, it's not that, Hugo. This is really a nice place, and Miss Fannie is really an old lady—er—I mean a nice old lady," she lied. "It's just that—well"—she gave me a quick look that told me not to interrupt—"it's just that Jan's homesick."

"But I thought her parents were in England," Hugo said.

"She's not homesick for them. She's"—Courtney was thinking hard—"she's homesick for—for her new pet, Calvin."

Before Courtney could continue, Denise burst through the swinging door. Denise must be one of those people who wake up grouchy in the morning, although, as far as I could tell, Denise was always grouchy.

"What in heaven's name was all that yelling about?" she yelled, poking an accusing finger at Courtney. "It's a good thing Miss Fannie doesn't have any neighbors on this island, Courtney. You could have raised the dead with that scream!"

As if to prove her point, William appeared. "Did I hear you call, Sir Junior?"

"No, it's nothing, William," Hugo said kindly to the old man. "Perhaps you can set the table. I am preparing breakfast for all of us."

William nodded and shuffled slowly out of the kitchen.

Hugo tried to calm Denise, who was still glaring at Courtney. "Courtney was explaining to me that her young friend is a bit homesick."

"Homesick!" Denise snorted contemptuously,

leering at me. "You've only been here eight hours."

Remembering that Courtney had said we shouldn't take no for an answer, I threw back my chin and said in a commanding voice, "Denise, I insist that you take me home today."

"You twerp!" Denise narrowed her eyes and gave me a menacing stare. "Who do you think you are to insist on anything? That goes for you too, Courtney. You're both twerps!"

"Now, now, my sweet one." Hugo hopped to her side and patted her shoulder. "That is no way to speak to young ladies. What Denise means," he explained kindly, "is that you are both punks, and it is impossible for us to take you back to the city today."

"Why is it impossible?" Courtney wanted an explanation.

Hugo and Denise glanced at each other. I could tell they were both trying to think of a reasonable answer to Courtney's question.

"You see, girls." Denise smiled sweetly and assumed her governess attitude. "Hugo and I have to work today."

Denise had about reached the end of her limited patience, but Courtney continued to press for answers. "Work, what kind of work?" she wanted to know.

"Besides being a psychiatrist, Hugo is also a writer. One day very soon now"—Denise raised her head proudly and flashed a smile at Hugo—"the name Hugo Malcalm will be as famous as that of William Shakespeare."

"Now, now, my sweet one." Hugo smiled modestly. "You see, young ladies, I am just putting the final touches to my latest play." He grinned broadly, forgetting to be modest. "I am certain that it will win the Pulitzer Prize." For some reason he suddenly frowned. "There is only one problem. It has been written with only one actress in mind. And I *must* have that actress in my play."

Denise kissed Hugo lightly on the cheek. "Now, darling, we're working on that problem right now, remember?"

Courtney and I exchanged a puzzled glance, not understanding.

"Now, young ladies," Hugo said, "you should go into the dining room, and in a few minutes I shall serve you cauliflower omelet à la Hugo."

Courtney and I went into the dining room. We both knew we had just taken no for an answer. There was no way we'd be leaving Miss Fannie's island today.

The dining-room table was the longest one I'd ever seen. There were six chairs on either side plus one chair at the foot of the table and one at the head. Courtney and I chose two chairs next to each other near the center of the table.

William was already seated on the opposite side of the table, to the left of the head chair. I guess setting the table for six people had worn him out. He sat with his head leaned against the high-backed chair. His mouth was open, and he snored softly.

Just as the grandfather clock in the next room indicated that it was eight-thirty, Miss Fannie entered the room and took her chair at the head of the table.

Now that Miss Fannie had her purple wig back on her head and about fifteen pounds of jewelry draped around her neck and wrists, she looked like an old queen taking charge of her throne. She reached for a sterling-silver dinner bell placed on the table in front of her. She rang it six or seven times. "Junior! Breakfast is to be served at eight-thirty sharp!"

"Yes, Granny." Hugo obediently entered, pushing a serving cart. He served Miss Fannie first. Miss Fannie squinted doubtfully at the cauliflower omelet before she unfolded a napkin and tucked it around her neck.

Denise seated herself as far away from Miss Fannie as possible. After Hugo finished serving everyone, he took his place at the foot of the table. He whipped open a napkin and placed it ceremoniously across his lap.

Courtney started to reach for her fork.

"Please." Hugo frowned. "First we shall say grace." We all lowered our heads as Hugo prayed. "Almighty One, we are thankful for this delicious omelet prepared by my own talented hands. Amen."

I hoped God would forgive Hugo for that lie because after the first bite of cauliflower omelet à la Hugo, I knew we weren't all that thankful. Courtney and I stared at each other, gulped, and reached for water. I drank a whole glassful before I was able to wash away that taste of burned cauliflower and raw eggs.

"Young ladies," Hugo said cordially, "I'm sure you will enjoy Miss Fannie's little island paradise. Denise and I will be busy working on the final revision of my play, but you both may spend the day exploring the island."

"Denise," Courtney said, "you know I never miss any episode of my favorite soap opera, 'Depressing Days of My Life.' Where is the television set?"

"That's why Miss Fannie's island is a paradise," Denise replied. "She permits no television, tele-phones, or newspapers here. It's like another world." She sighed. "So peaceful and serene."

Courtney looked stricken. "But today Emily's third husband is returning after nine years in prison. This is probably going to be the most important depressing day of Emily's whole life. I just *can't* miss the program today."

Denise was not concerned with the problems of either Courtney or Emily. "Why don't you and Jan go down to the beach and build sand castles?"

"Sand castles," Courtney muttered under her breath as she pushed away from the table.

We returned to the upstairs room.

Courtney collapsed on the bed and continued to mutter. "What a dump. No telephone—no radio—no television."

I smiled and walked to the closet. I carried my overnight bag to the bed and placed it next to Courtney. "I have a surprise for you, Courtney." Like a magician pulling a rabbit out of a hat, I pulled my new portable television out of my suitcase.

"Allright, Jan!" Courtney suddenly perked up. "You don't know how important 'Depressing Days of My Life' is to me. Sometimes I feel as though Emily is my best friend. I feel sorry for her. She's had a lot of bad luck."

Courtney propped herself up against the headboard, balanced the television on her knees, and flipped it on. I sat next to her.

"We're really lucky, Jan. The show is just starting." Courtney's eyes were glued to the screen.

A lady paced back and forth across her living room. She stopped, lit a cigarette, and started to pace the floor again. Organ music played softly, sadly, in the background. The lady stopped pacing and sat down on a sofa. She crushed her cigarette into an ashtray. She poured herself a cup of coffee from the beautiful silver service that just happened to be on the coffee table in front of her. It was plain to see that the lady was really nervous. The doorbell rang. The lady jumped up.

Courtney sat up expectantly. "That's Emily's third husband at the door. Poor Emily, she's had a lot of bad luck. I sure hope everything's going to work out for her this time."

Suddenly the TV picture went dark. A voice said, "Ladies and gentlemen, we interrupt our regularly scheduled program to bring you this exclusive special report."

"What! They can't do that," Courtney said indignantly. "Emily's husband is at the front door."

When the TV picture returned, it was of a newscaster seated behind a desk. He was very solemn. "We have just received word that Courtney Van Allen, millionaire cereal heiress, was abducted from her grandmother's penthouse in Manhattan at approximately ten o'clock last night. Miss Van Allen, age twelve, is the daughter of California Senator James Van Allen and actress Sylvia Sutton. For some months Miss Van Allen has been living with her grandmother, Isabelle Van Allen, in Manhattan. Mrs. Van Allen resides in the penthouse of this Fifth Avenue apartment building."

A slide of the Fifth Avenue Central Park Tower appeared on the screen behind the announcer. As the announcer continued, the screen started flashing pictures of Courtney: Courtney when she was a baby, Courtney when she posed for the Courtney Crummies cereal box, Courtney when she started kindergarten, Courtney in a ballet class, Courtney ice-skating in Rockefeller Plaza, Courtney skiing in Colorado, Courtney taking tennis lessons in Palm Springs. I waited for Courtney to appear in her "drop dead" clothes, but she never did. I guess Mrs. Van Allen had never allowed anyone to take Courtney's picture after she became a dropout.

"We have learned that Senator Van Allen in Washington and Sylvia Sutton in California are at this moment making arrangements to fly to New York. We will have further details of the kidnapping at noon. We now return you to our regularly scheduled program."

As the announcer signed off, a cold, tight knot of fear gripped the inside of my stomach.

Courtney had turned chalk white. Her eyes were wide as she whispered the terrifying word "kidnapped."

seven

VEN though I hadn't been
mentioned in the news report, having learned that I
was a kidnap victim had a weakening effect on me. I
felt helpless and frightened. The same news had a
different effect on Courtney.

Courtney snapped off the television and leaped
from the bed. "Don't worry, Jan," she reassured
me. "We're going to break out of here." She paced
back and forth across the room, mumbling more to
herself than to me. "Don't worry, I'll figure out
something."

A cold knot of terror gripped my insides, but I
was smart enough to know that I couldn't give in to
panic. Things didn't look too good, but Courtney
and I had to keep our wits about us.

We concentrated for a long time, trying to come

up with some plan of escape. I found myself thinking about my parents. Did they know yet that I had been kidnapped? Had Aunt Harry called them in London?

Courtney interrupted my thoughts. "You know what I don't understand? Why is Hugo doing this? Do you know how much money my grandmother pays him every time I go to his office? Seventy-five dollars! Dozens of rich kids in this city are his patients. One kid even jets in his father's plane all the way from Dallas, Texas, to meet with Hugo every Saturday afternoon."

"And don't forget Miss Fannie," I reminded her. "Hugo's grandmother owns this whole island. You're right, Courtney. Hugo has to be rich. He must have some other reason for kidnapping you."

"Like what?" Courtney wanted to know.

"I don't know. We'll just have to tune in at noon. The announcer said they'd have further details on our kidnapping then. In the meantime," I said decisively, "we'd better hide the television set and pretend that we don't know anything." I carried the TV back to the closet and closed the door.

"You're right," Courtney agreed. "We'll keep the TV out of sight and pretend we don't know we've been kidnapped." Then she did a strange thing; she started undressing.

"What are you doing?" I asked in dismay.

Courtney tossed her "drop dead" T-shirt onto the floor. "Get me my pajamas, will you, Jan?" She dropped her jeans in a heap next to the T-shirt.

I went into the bathroom and picked her pajamas up off the floor. "What are you doing?" I repeated, handing her the pajamas.

"What does it look like? I'm getting ready for bed," Courtney explained patiently.

"At eleven o'clock in the morning?"

She ignored my question, buttoned the pajamas, climbed into bed, and slipped in between the bed covers.

"All right, Jan," she said, adjusting the pillow behind her head. "Here's my plan. I'm going to play sick."

I nodded and waited for her to continue. "Well?" I finally said.

"Well, what?"

"Courtney," I said in exasperation, "is that your whole plan? You're going to play sick?"

Courtney narrowed her eyes and said defensively, "Do you have a better idea?"

"Well, no," I had to admit. "I don't have any ideas right now, but how is getting sick going to get us back to New York City?"

"I am the daughter of a great actress, Jan," Courtney said proudly, evidently forgetting the number of times she had said she thought her mother stank. "All my life I've known that I was going to grow up to be either an actress or a senator. I haven't decided yet which one I want to be. But right now I'm going to play a great scene," she promised. "When I get through, Hugo and Denise won't think I'm just sick, they'll think I'm dying."

"And you think you can get them to take you to a doctor or to a hospital?" I said, starting to understand her plan.

"Exactly," Courtney nodded confidently. "But I need your help, Jan."

"What can I do?" I sat on the edge of the bed and listened carefully as Courtney lowered her voice and told me my part in the Great Escape.

"Here's what you do, Jan. Sneak down to Denise's room and bring back a tube of lipstick."

"Lipstick!"

"Shh!" Courtney warned. "Yes, lipstick. I'll smear some on my face so that I'll look flushed, as if I'm running a high fever."

"Courtney, do you really think this is going to work?" I asked doubtfully.

Courtney lifted her head with confidence and pride. "Sylvia Sutton is my mother. I've studied her acting techniques."

She seemed to consider these statements an adequate answer to my question. I wanted to hear more about the acting techniques she was planning to use, but there was no time to waste.

As I headed out the door, Courtney called softly, "Be careful, Jan."

I descended the stairs as silently as a cat. When I reached the second level, I looked up and down the long corridor. I crept to the bannister and leaned over to get a view into the entry hall below. No one was in sight. The house was so still that the only sound I could hear was the beating of my own heart. I made my way cautiously to Denise's room. The door was partially open. I slipped in and closed the door behind me. My heart was pounding faster now, and I thought my ears would burst with each deafening beat. I checked the bathroom first. My eyes quickly darted around the room. A pair of panty hose dangled over the side of the tub. A damp towel was lying in a heap next to the shower. Denise had all kinds of makeup spread all over the sink counter, but no lipstick.

I went back into the bedroom and was about to check the top of the dresser when I spotted Denise's purse on a chair near the closet. I hesitated a moment. I had never before looked through someone else's purse. I had never before stolen anything. But this was different. This was a matter of life and death. With that thought in mind, I unzipped the large leather bag. Lying on the very top was a gun!

I shuddered, but I carefully lifted the gun from the purse, holding the handle between two fingers and making certain that the barrel was pointed toward the floor.

Holding the gun in one hand, I rummaged through the purse until I found what I was looking for. I removed a tube of lipstick called Ripe Tomato, closed the purse, and placed it on the chair exactly as I had found it when I heard footsteps coming down the hallway. I had no time to think. Instinctively, I darted inside the closet and hid behind a long robe.

A second later Denise entered the room. I could hear her humming a verse of "Old McDonald Had a Farm" to herself. Her footsteps sounded as if they were coming toward the closet. I pressed myself tightly against the wall. My heart was hammering so fast that I was afraid it might explode.

Denise started to sing, ". . . and on that farm he had a pig" when I heard the bathroom door close. If I was going to get out of there it had to be now! Silently I opened the door and tiptoed across the room. I glanced at the closed bathroom door. As I left Denise's room I could clearly hear her loud soprano singing, *E-I-E-I-O—*"

I probably broke the world's sprinting record returning to the upstairs room. I nearly gave Courtney a heart attack as I burst into the room holding a gun in one hand and the tube of lipstick in the other. "You'll never believe it," I panted, trying to catch my breath.

"What? What happened?" Courtney didn't take her eyes off the gun.

"Denise—she came back—I had to hide in the closet."

"Oh, my gosh!" Courtney whispered. "Did she see you?"

"No." I shook my head, still trying to catch my

breath. "She was too busy singing 'Old McDonald Had a Farm.'"

Courtney nodded. "That's one of her favorites."

"I'm going to hide the gun in the closet with the TV set," I told her. "We don't want any violence."

I was relieved to see that Courtney agreed with me. "We won't need the gun. My plan can't fail."

One thing I admire about Courtney is her confidence. I hid the gun and then handed Courtney the tube of lipstick.

Opening the tube of Ripe Tomato, she said, "Now I know they're going to believe I'm really sick."

Courtney went into the bathroom and applied the lipstick first to her face and then to her neck and chest and arms. "You see, Jan," she explained, "I've watched professional Hollywood makeup men change my mother into anything the script called for many times."

"Yeah," I said, suddenly remembering one of my favorite Sylvia Sutton shows. "Once your mother had to go under cover to expose an old-age nursing home. She was made up to look eighty years old."

"Remember the time my mother got shot on the show?"

"Which time? Your mother gets shot practically every week, Courtney."

"I know. She usually gets grazed in the arm or leg. But I mean the time she was critically wounded: shot twice, both bullets lodged close to the heart. You almost thought she was really going to die that time—until the last five minutes of the program. Well, I was there in the studio when my mom filmed that show. I know that certain way she has of sighing and moaning in pain."

Courtney smeared the finishing touches of lipstick in a sickening-looking blotch on her stomach! She closed the tube and handed it back to me. "We'd better hide this with the gun and the TV." She looked at herself approvingly in the mirror. Her eyes sparkled as she smiled at her own sickly image. "I feel pretty good now, Jan, but by the time I make it back to bed, I'm going to be dying."

In less than an instant an amazing change took place in Courtney. Her eyes became glazed and dull. Her mouth tightened with pain, and her shoulders sagged. She walked across the room in agony. She lowered herself into bed and let her head fall back against the pillow in sheer exhaustion. I had never been so impressed by any performance in my life.

"Courtney," I said, standing over her, "you're an even better actress than your mother. Hugo and Denise really are going to think you're sick."

"One more thing, Jan," Courtney whispered bravely through the pain, as if she were about to make a final request. "Bring me a hot washcloth and a glass of hot water. Let the water run really hot."

When I returned from the bathroom, Courtney put the glass under the bed and slapped the washcloth on her head. I silently watched steam rise up above her covered face. When she removed the cloth, the effect was complete. Drops of water ran down her cheeks, making it appear that she was perspiring and literally burning up with a fever.

"All right, Jan," she ordered. "Go get Hugo and Denise!"

I crashed out the door and bolted down the stairs two at a time. I yelled hysterically, "Hugo! Denise!" I continued shouting all the way down to the main floor. I thought I heard voices coming from the library. I banged on the door. I didn't wait for an answer but pushed my way in and screamed, "Hugo! Denise! Come quick!"

Hugo was pacing the floor, dictating dialogue from his play to Denise. From their expressions I could see that I had successfully alarmed both of them.

Hugo took one hop toward me. "What is it, young lady? What is wrong?"

"It's Courtney! She's—I'm not sure, but I think she's DYING!" I ended on a hysterical note and charged back upstairs. I could hear them tearing up the stairs after me. I congratulated myself on my own performance. When I reached Courtney's bedside, Hugo and Denise were running right behind me.

Hugo pushed me aside and bent over Courtney. She lay very still.

With great effort she somehow managed to lift her heavy eyelids. Her lips moved, but no words came out. Finally she was able to whisper one word: "Hugo?"

Hugo had to bend closer to hear her. "Yes, my child," he said kindly, filled with concern. "It is I." At the same time he placed the palm of his hand on Courtney's forehead. "*Eek!* She is on fire!"

Hugo screeched out this information in such a shrill, piercing voice that everyone in the room, including Courtney, jumped. Courtney quickly lowered her head and moaned softly.

"Denise, my sweet one," Hugo said with great anxiety. "Quickly get a thermometer!"

Within minutes Denise returned. Hugo took the thermometer, carefully shook it, and placed it under Courtney's tongue.

During the time it took to take Courtney's temperature, Denise and Hugo had moved over by the window. I purposely stood by the bed near Courtney so that I could block her from their view. As I stood there she quickly yanked the thermometer from her mouth, leaned over, and dipped it in the glass of hot water. When she heard Hugo's hopping footsteps behind me, she whipped the thermometer back into her mouth.

Hugo bent over to remove the thermometer. He said reassuringly, "Now do not worry, my child. You are going to be fine." At the same time he glanced at the thermometer. "*Eek!*" He slapped the palm of his hand against his forehead in horror. "One hundred and five! She is DYING."

"Hugo—" Courtney whispered pathetically.

"Yes, yes, my child," said Hugo, trying to calm down. "What is it?"

"Hugo." Before she could continue, Courtney moaned, trying bravely not to let her suffering show. "Hugo, please—I need a doctor."

Hugo agreed. "That is why you are very fortunate."

"Fortunate?" Courtney repeated through a painful sigh.

"You see, my child," Hugo explained, reaching inside the medical bag, "I *am* a doctor."

"But, Hugo," Courtney said weakly, "I don't mean a psychiatrist, I mean a medical doctor."

"Yes, that is correct. Like every psychiatrist, I am also an M.D."

In her surprise, Courtney forgot how sick she was supposed to be. She started to sit up. "You're a *real* doctor?"

Even Denise seemed to be concerned over Courtney's poor health. She frowned and placed the back of her hand against Courtney's damp cheek. "She's so flushed, Hugo. Do you suppose your omelet made her ill?"

Hugo stared at Denise as if he couldn't believe what he'd just heard.

"No," Denise continued, unaware of Hugo's shocked expression, "that couldn't be it. After all, the rest of us managed to eat it and somehow survive. But just to make sure, Hugo, I think we need to clean out this child's insides. What she needs is a good enema!" Denise promptly marched into the bathroom in search of the equipment necessary for her medical recommendation.

I was so hypnotized by Courtney's bulging eyeballs that I didn't realize that Denise had left the bathroom and was heading for the closet.

Then everything happened at once. Courtney leaped to the center of the bed, where she stood clutching the bedclothes to her. Her face, already the shade of a ripe tomato, turned purple as she shouted, "HUGO! DENISE! I'M WELL!"

At the same instant, Denise, standing just inside the closet, screamed, "What's this?"

"A miraculous recovery," Hugo replied, staring up at Courtney.

"No, Hugo, I mean *this*." Denise charged angrily out of the closet, carrying the TV set and the tube of lipstick in one hand. She held the gun in her other hand, carelessly waving it about in her rage. "Don't you see, Hugo?" She stuck the gun practically under his nose. "These twerps have been in my purse."

"Now, sweet one"—Hugo cautiously took the gun from Denise—"calm down."

"Calm down!" Denise stamped her foot and glared first at Courtney and then at me. "Look at this!" She opened the almost empty tube of lipstick. "Do you know how much Ripe Tomato costs!"

From her standing position in the middle of the

bed Courtney shouted, "Jan and I know we've been kidnapped! We were going to blast our way out of here! And even if you did find the gun, that's not going to stop us! We'll just find another way to blast our way out of here!"

Hugo hopped about, trying to calm everyone. "I am a psychiatrist. It is my profession to help people control their emotions." He threw his hands help-lessly into the air and shouted, "EVERYONE CONTROL YOUR EMOTIONS!"

We all sat down.

"Now then," Hugo said, taking full charge. "It appears that you young ladies have learned that you have been kidnapped. The word *kidnapped* is prob-ably a frightening word, especially if one is a kid. But let me assure you"—he gave both Courtney and me a kind smile—"no harm shall come to you. I have never harmed a child—not even that disgusting wimp Gerald Norman, who flies to my office from Texas every Saturday. So you see"—he shrugged and hopped once—"you are in no danger at all."

"Hugo," my voice was shaking, "why did you kidnap us?"

Denise answered for him. I was surprised to hear her speak in an almost gentle tone. "We didn't want to kidnap you, Jan. You just happened to be with Courtney at the time we planned to bring her to Miss Fannie's island."

"Well, I hope you don't expect to get too much money for me." Courtney's eyes filled with tears. "I don't think my parents will care if they get me back or not." She swallowed and wiped her eyes with the back of her hand. Some of the Ripe Tomato smeared across her nose and cheek.

"Well, what do you expect, Courtney?" Denise's irritable tone returned. "You're rude, you're insulting, and you looked completely ridiculous marching around in that stupid 'drop dead' suit for the last forty days."

"Forty-nine days," Courtney corrected.

"Forty-nine days," Denise repeated. "Anyway, Hugo's not asking your parents for money."

Courtney looked at Hugo. "What my sweet one says is true. I do not plan to demand money from your parents, Courtney. Although I am quite certain that both your mother and your father love you a great deal and would pay any amount for your safe return."

The look on Courtney's face softened as she tried to blink away fresh tears.

Hugo bent closer to Courtney. He sounded like the wisest, most sympathetic psychiatrist in the world. "My dear Courtney, I do not want you to think of yourself as being kidnapped. As I have explained, I am not asking for money. I am asking for an exchange."

Courtney blinked. "An exchange?"

"You will be returned when your mother agrees to meet with me."

Courtney was amazed. "That's all? You just want

to meet my mother?" Courtney uncrossed her legs and slid off the bed. She planted her feet firmly on the floor and stared Hugo straight in the eye. "You mean you brought us all the way out here to this island in the middle of the Atlantic Ocean just so you could meet my mother?"

"We've told you, neither of you has anything to worry about. Just as soon as your mother agrees to come out to Miss Fannie's island, you'll both be returned," said Denise. She took Hugo by the arm. "Come, darling, let's leave the children alone for a while."

At the door, Hugo paused and spoke as a very considerate host to his guests. "I do not wish for you young ladies to feel like prisoners here at Miss Fannie's. Please make yourselves at home and feel free to explore the island."

After they left, Courtney and I moved about aimlessly in the huge playroom. We remained silent, each of us thinking. I thought about my parents and Aunt Harry. I thought about my home in California and my friends there. I thought about Hugo, Denise, Miss Fannie, Sylvia Sutton, and the whole strange situation I was in the middle of.

After a long while Courtney said, "Well, what now?"

I had been leaning against the window sill, staring out at the beach. "I think we should do what Hugo suggested. Let's explore the island."

eight

Courtney went into the bathroom to wash off the Ripe Tomato and change back into her "drop dead" clothes. At the last minute I decided to take my portable television set along on our tour of the island.

We decided to investigate the western end of the island first. Along the way we stopped to admire a garden alive with all varieties of beautiful flowers and decided there must be a gardener on the island. We found a small cottage near the edge of the garden. Its doors were locked, and we could find no one about.

We continued on until we came to the stables. We pushed open the double doors, expecting to find nothing but deserted stalls.

"Look, Courtney!" A chestnut mare greeted us

with a whinny and a shake of her head. In the stall next to her was an almost identical horse.

Courtney seemed to like horses as much as I did. We petted both mares for a long while. They were well groomed, and their stalls were filled with fresh straw and water.

"I don't get it, Jan. Miss Fannie must have a lot of people working for her on this island. I wonder where everyone is."

"I bet Hugo had them sent away when he decided to bring us here."

"Yeah," Courtney agreed. "He wouldn't want a lot of people around to be witnesses to his kidnapping."

We gave the horses a final pat and headed thoughtfully toward a bridle trail.

"Jan, I've been thinking about my mother." Courtney's frown and the quiet of her voice showed that she was deeply concerned. "What could be important enough to make Hugo kidnap me just so he could force my mother to come to this island?"

"Your mother must be his favorite actress in the whole world," I said, recalling the theater we had seen earlier. "That theater is like a shrine to Fannie Violet and Sylvia Sutton."

"I know," Courtney replied. "That's what worries me. He has all of my mother's movies and posters. Maybe what he wants now is my mother. He might want to keep her locked up in the theater or something crazy like that. Jan, there's only one thing to do." She squared her shoulders. "We've got to save her. We have to get off this island before Hugo can exchange me for my mother."

"I thought you didn't like your mother, Courtney. You told me she stinks."

"After my parents separated, I thought they didn't love me anymore. So I decided to stop loving them too." Courtney's words were barely above a whisper, and she was explaining more to herself than to me. "Plenty of things still stink, Jan," Courtney said gruffly, unable to completely drop her dropout act. "But," she said in a softer tone, "not my mother. She's really neat."

I smiled to myself because I always suspected that Courtney really loved her mother.

We had just reached the far end of the island. The afternoon had turned cloudy and cool. The sky was the color of steel, and the water was gray and choppy and not very inviting.

Courtney stared out across the ocean toward Long Island, concentrating so deeply that I could practically hear her thinking. I could tell another plan was forming in her brain. I only hoped it would be better than the last one.

"Are you a good swimmer?" she asked.

I carefully considered the question. "I'm pretty good."

She continued to stare at the Long Island shore. "It's only three miles across."

I carefully considered the angry waves that

slapped against the beach. "I'm probably more of an average swimmer."

We had a long discussion about it. At last we agreed that neither of us was a strong enough swimmer to chance the rough waters between Miss Fannie's island and Long Island. We also considered the currents that could pull us out into the open ocean. And with the heavy mist that was pouring in, it was possible that the entire area would soon be covered with fog. It was just too risky.

From the western tip of the island we headed back across the wet sand to the pier near the front of the mansion where the boats were anchored. Hugo's speedboat couldn't be of any help to us because he had the key, so we decided to investigate the *Miss Fannie*.

Walking along highly polished wooden decks, we managed to peek into a living room, a lounge with a bar, a galley, and two bedrooms. Every room on the yacht was locked, but we continued toward the captain's cabin hoping that if we could get inside we might be able to radio for help.

As we figured, the cabin turned out to be locked. Courtney seriously considered breaking one of the windows with a croquet mallet, but we both decided that the radio equipment looked too complicated for us to understand, so we left the yacht.

There were three main paths that led from the pier. We chose one that led to a gazebo situated on a knoll in the center of the front yard. The gazebo was filled with white wrought-iron furniture. I placed my TV set on a table and pulled out a chair. Courtney plopped, weary and miserable, into a chair next to me. At exactly noon I turned on the news.

"Following this message of interest, we will bring you the latest developments in the Courtney Van Allen kidnapping case," the announcer promised.

The "message of interest" proved to be three commercials. The first one was about which soap could get your clothes the whitest; the second explained why, if you loved your dog, you would always feed him Tony's Bonies; and the third showed a woman spraying her armpits. The "message of interest" ended, and a solemn-looking announcer reappeared on the screen.

"Last night, at approximately ten o'clock, Courtney Van Allen was abducted from her grandmother's Fifth Avenue penthouse. At the time of her disappearance, she was accompanied by her governess, Denise Abbott, age thirty-five, and a young friend." In the silence that followed, the announcer could be heard to whisper to his TV crew, "What's her name?"

I swallowed hard to keep from crying. On the first broadcast I wasn't even mentioned, and now I was called "What's-her-name?" If I wasn't even important enough for them to find out my name, was I important enough for them to try to rescue? It was a good thing I was with Courtney. Every policeman, every FBI agent, probably the whole world, was searching for her.

The announcer fumbled with some papers on his desk. "Yes. Courtney was accompanied by her governess and a friend, Jan Travis, also age twelve."

I had been twelve years old for only one day, and already I was wondering if I'd live long enough to reach my teens.

"We have here in the studio Senator Van Allen, who has just arrived in New York from Washington. He is here to make a special plea to the kidnappers for his daughter's safety."

The camera moved in on a man seated next to the announcer. Senator Van Allen looked about the same age as my father. He had dark hair that was just beginning to show traces of gray around the temples. His forehead was lined with deep wrinkles of concern. He looked very serious and very worried. When he spoke, his voice was deep and steady. "I don't know who you are or what it is you want. What I do know is that you have the most precious thing in the world to me: my daughter."

The senator's steady voice faltered. He swallowed and continued. "I was having breakfast with the President of the United States this morning when I first received news of the abduction. The President has personally spoken with the head of the FBI, and they assure me that everything possible is being done to locate Courtney.

"Wherever you are, I beg you to please contact

me. Your demands will be met. I ask in return that you please not harm my little girl."

The senator fought hard to control his voice. "Courtney, if you are watching, know that we are doing everything possible for your safe return and the safe return of your friend." The senator paused, not able to recall my name. Now I was getting mad. Surely a United States senator should be smart enough to remember a simple name like Jan.

Turning to the announcer, Senator Van Allen whispered, "What's her name?" Looking back into the camera, he continued, ". . . your friend, Jan Travis. Courtney, I love you. I promise you'll be safe soon."

Tears streamed down Courtney's face. She wiped them away with the back of her hand.

"Our control unit is standing by at Kennedy Airport for the arrival of Courtney Van Allen's mother, actress Sylvia Sutton."

The picture switched over to an airport waiting room. The small room was jammed with dozens of reporters, and cameras and other equipment. The reporter for our station held a microphone close to his mouth and spoke in an excited voice.

"Ladies and gentlemen, Sylvia Sutton's plane arrived here only moments ago. She should be walking through that door at any second."

A cry went up from everyone as Sylvia Sutton entered. She looked almost as good as she did when she is playing the role of the girl reporter on her

TV series. Only on the series she's always smiling, cool and confident. Now she looked close to tears. A microphone was pushed under her nose.

"Miss Sutton, can you tell us where you were when you received the news about Courtney?"

"I was in Hollywood filming my series. Please, if you don't mind"—she tried to push through the crowd—"I only want to get my *baby*." The word came out in a sob. "Mama's coming. You're going to be all right."

This was too much for Courtney. She buried her face in her hands and cried. I found a Kleenex in my pocket and handed it to her. I didn't know what to say because I felt like crying too.

The TV cameras showed the back of Sylvia pushing through a crowded corridor. The announcer returned. "We shall have more about the Van Allen kidnapping after this word of importance."

"This word of importance" turned out to be three commercials: a cereal commercial, not Courtney Crummies; a can with a picture of a peach on the outside, which was supposed to be sprayed once a week in the bathroom bowl; and a special foot powder to use in case you wanted your feet to smell like perfume.

During the commercial break, I glanced back at the house. Hugo and Denise had told us they didn't have a television set, but now I wondered if they had been lying. Senator Van Allen's message had been for them. They needed some way to keep up with what was happening. I decided that they must even have a phone hidden in there someplace. I was about to discuss this with Courtney when the news came back on, with *my* picture on the screen behind the announcer!

It was a picture taken over two years ago when I had been in the fourth grade. It was the worst picture I ever had taken in my entire nine years. My own mother refused to pay the photographer for a job she had described as "putrid." The first time a picture of me had ever been shown on national television, and they had to show *that one!* I resolved that if I ever got out of this mess, the first thing I'd do was to give Aunt Harry a more recent picture of myself.

"Jan Travis, the twelve-year-old child who was abducted with Courtney Van Allen, is the daughter of Dr. and Mrs. Benjamin Travis of Monterey, California. At the time of the kidnapping, Miss Travis was staying with her aunt, Harriet Petrie. Mrs. Petrie and Isabelle Van Allen, Courtney's grandmother, live in the same Manhattan apartment building.

"According to our latest reports, Dr. and Mrs. Travis have been notified of the kidnapping. They are at present en route to New York from London, where the doctor was attending a medical convention."

I knew my mother and father would be frantic with worry. I wanted somehow to let them know I was all right. I closed my eyes and thought as hard as I could, hoping to transfer my thoughts to them through mental telepathy. I never really believed in telepathy, but right then anything seemed worth a try.

I was just about to turn the TV off when the announcer said, "I have seated next to me Harriet Petrie. Mrs. Petrie is the great-aunt of Jan Travis, the child kidnapped along with Courtney Van Allen."

I adjusted the TV set on my knees and gave Aunt Harry my full attention. Courtney blew her nose, shifted her position, and waited expectantly to hear what Aunt Harry had to say. As usual, Aunt Harry had plenty to say.

"Mrs. Petrie," the announcer said as the camera moved in for a close-up of Aunt Harry, "could you tell us—"

"I am here," she interrupted, "to talk to the kidnapper, whoever he may be. Stealing children away from their homes in the middle of the night! You should be ashamed! It's *disgraceful!*" Aunt Harry glared threateningly into the camera. "I'm here to tell you I don't know what you want and I don't care. What I do care about are the two children you have stolen away from the families that love them. I want you to know that my niece is one of the loveliest girls in the world." Aunt Harry glanced fondly at the large picture of me that was still on the screen behind her. She looked back into the camera and said apologetically, "Although I must admit that awful picture doesn't begin to do her justice. Jan, if you're watching—"

"Mrs. Petrie," the announcer said, trying to get Aunt Harry to focus on his prepared questions, "could you tell us—"

Aunt Harry completely ignored him. She spoke directly into the camera; it was almost as if she were talking only to me. "As I was saying, pet, your parents are arriving at the airport at three this afternoon."

The announcer cleared his throat and said in a more forceful tone, "Mrs. Petrie, PLEASE—"

"Young man, kindly stop interrupting me!" demanded Aunt Harry. "I have one more thing I'd like to say—"

"Folks." The announcer sounded desperate. He leaned over in front of Aunt Harry and shouted, "WE'LL RETURN RIGHT AFTER THIS COMMERCIAL MESSAGE!"

Only the announcer returned after the commercial. Aunt Harry was nowhere in sight. The news about the kidnapping was over. In place of where my picture had been was a weather map.

Courtney blew her nose again and managed a half-grin. "I like your aunt, Jan. She sure gave Hugo a piece of her mind."

"Just think, Courtney, the President of the United States is working on our case."

"Yeah," Courtney replied, obviously not overly

impressed by this fact. "He's a friend of my father's."

"Really?" I said in awe. "Have you met the President?"

"Yes," she replied matter-of-factly. "Once I had lunch at the White House with him and his family."

"Weren't you nervous? I mean, what do you say to the President of the United States?"

Courtney shrugged. "I said, 'Pass the salt, please.'"

We sat in the gazebo for a long while, watching the ocean and doing a lot of reflective thinking about ourselves and our families. We hadn't turned off the TV set, and every now and then I became aware of some lady on a game show jumping up and down like crazy. After a while, another contestant started screaming hysterically when she was told she'd won four wire-wheel hubcaps and ten cases of tuna fish. She started kissing the host of the show until he had to grab one of the hubcaps and use it as a shield to protect himself.

At one o'clock we headed back to the house. Hugo served us fruit and cottage cheese for lunch. He apologized for not preparing something more elaborate. I thought we were lucky, because even Hugo couldn't ruin fruit and cottage cheese.

After lunch, Courtney and I returned to the upstairs playroom, where we spent the remainder of the day. I was about midway through a novel

I'd found in Hugo's childhood library when Courtney finally stopped pacing about. She carried my TV set into the sitting-room area, sighed, and sank into an easy chair.

"Jan, it's time for the five o'clock news."

I carefully marked my spot in the book and joined Courtney. The lead news story was about the kidnapping of Courtney Van Allen. The same pictures we had seen on the earlier broadcast were flashed across the screen. We listened intently for some new information.

"We now switch you to our on-the-spot reporter, Steve Lance, who is standing by inside the Van Allen penthouse, where Courtney Van Allen was abducted late last night."

Courtney and I both squinted and leaned closer to the tiny TV screen. When on-the-spot reporter Steve Lance came on the screen, I immediately recognized the Van Allen living room. Steve Lance was sitting in the same chair where I had sat only a few days ago when I had gone with Aunt Harry to meet Courtney.

As Steve Lance spoke into a mini microphone clipped to his necktie, the camera moved to a couch where Senator Van Allen sat next to Sylvia Sutton. The senator held Sylvia's hand as he answered one of Lance's questions.

"That's correct," Courtney's father said. "We did receive a message from the kidnapper. At three o'clock this afternoon, a man who would identify himself only as 'Junior' asked to speak to my wife. He made it clear that he's not demanding money but that he wants to meet with and talk to Sylvia."

"Miss Sutton," Lance asked, "do you plan to meet with this man who calls himself 'Junior'?"

Very often in her movies, and especially on her TV series, Sylvia Sutton has to pretend to be tense and under a great strain. Only now she wasn't pretending. For the first time, I noticed that Sylvia had wrinkles across her forehead and dark circles under her eyes. But she was still very beautiful as she answered bravely, "Of course. I plan to do whatever I need to do to see that Courtney is returned safely."

"This appears to be a highly unusual kidnapping case. You said 'Junior' hasn't demanded any ransom. He wants only to meet with you. Did he say what he wants to discuss with you?"

"No," Sylvia replied in her soft voice, "he didn't. He said that he would contact me tomorrow and give me further details then. He did assure me that Courtney and her friend, er . . ."

Not again, I thought. Even a great actress like Sylvia Sutton, who has to memorize pages of dialogue at a time, couldn't remember a simple three-letter name. As I was busy being annoyed, I heard my name being whispered to Sylvia. I recognized my mother's voice!

"Yes—Jan," Sylvia repeated. "I was assured that

both girls are well and safe." Sylvia looked straight into the camera. "I don't know if Courtney is watching or not. But if you are watching, Courtney, please remember how much Daddy and I love you." Tears filled Sylvia's famous blue eyes. She choked back a sob. "You'll be home soon, darling. I promise."

"Thank you, Miss Sutton," Steve Lance said in a sympathetic voice. Then with a wide smile he reminded the TV audience that he was in the Van Allen apartment, where Courtney Van Allen had been kidnapped. "We have just heard the latest details of what is developing in the Van Allen case. Also here with us are Dr. and Mrs. Travis. They are the parents of the twelve-year-old child who was taken along with Courtney."

I sat bolt upright, waiting for my parents to come into view. Instead, the studio anchorman appeared smiling from behind his desk. "Stay tuned, folks," he said happily. "After this brief message we will return with sports and details about this afternoon's Yankee game."

My parents were right there, and I didn't even get to see them. I blinked away tears. When I could see clearly again, I realized that Courtney was sobbing. Hugo's giant playroom had everything but a box of Kleenex, so I went into the bathroom and returned with a roll of toilet paper, which I handed to Courtney. Courtney ripped off long sections of the tissue, blew her nose several times, gave one big hiccup, and sat back in her chair. Then she did a strange thing: She smiled.

"They really love me," she said.

"Sure they do, Courtney," I replied. "You heard your mother say she was going to do whatever Hugo asks to get you back."

"I know." Courtney hiccupped again. "That's why we've got to figure some way to get off this island, Jan. I want to save my mom from being caged in Miss Fannie's movie theater."

Dinner was to be served at exactly six-thirty. We were in our places when Miss Fannie and William hobbled in together. They were dressed very formally: William in a tuxedo and Miss Fannie in a long purple dress with bunches of white lace around the neck and sleeves that had yellowed with age.

"Young ladies," Miss Fannie said after she caught her breath from the effort of sitting down, "I'm glad to see that you are punctual." She squinted at Courtney through wire-rimmed spectacles. "I don't understand this new custom of wearing clothes that serve as walking billboards." She peered closer to Courtney. "I can't see as well as I used to. What do you have written on your shirt, child?"

"Drop dead," Courtney replied.

Miss Fannie gasped. "Why, I never . . ." She started to sputter indignantly.

"Excuse me, Miss Fannie," Courtney said politely. "You asked me what was written on my shirt. That's what my shirt says: 'Drop dead.'"

This explanation didn't appease Miss Fannie. "Do you realize that I am ninety-eight years old? And William is *really* old! He's ninety-nine! Now how do you think those words make him feel?"

We all looked at William, who was leaning back against his chair, taking a short nap.

Just as the grandfather clock chimed six-thirty, Hugo and Denise entered. Between the two of them they managed in a single trip to arrange the entire dinner on the center of the table. Everything looked delicious, and I suddenly realized how hungry I was.

I noticed Miss Fannie look at her food. "Who did the cooking?" she demanded to know.

"I did, Granny," Hugo answered.

Miss Fannie bowed her head and crossed herself before stabbing at a veal cutlet with her fork. Her false teeth seemed to be getting in the way of her chewing, but somehow she managed. "When will you be returning to the city, Junior?"

"I have an important rendezvous in the city at six o'clock tomorrow evening, Granny," Hugo replied.

Courtney and I exchanged a knowing look. Hugo was planning to meet Sylvia Sutton at six o'clock tomorrow night!

Because of Miss Fannie's problem with her false teeth, and because William had to be awakened several times to be reminded to eat, dinner took nearly an hour. When Miss Fannie was finished, she folded her napkin on the table and reached up to adjust her purple hair, which had tilted slightly to one side during the meal, so that it balanced properly on the center of her head.

"Junior, did you inform our young guests about this evening's entertainment?" Miss Fannie's face cracked into a gracious smile that was directed at Courtney and me.

Denise almost pushed her chair over backward in her rush to depart. She spoke rapidly, putting on an expression of regret. "I'm afraid I'll have to miss this evening's entertainment, Miss Fannie."

Miss Fannie's watery blue eyes narrowed suspiciously. "And what do you have to attend to, missy?"

"I have to do the dishes and"—Denise was thinking hard for a good excuse—"I really must wash my hair tonight." She stacked several plates and rushed with them into the kitchen.

"Well, Junior, don't just sit there!" Miss Fannie reached for her cane and pounded it on the floor.

Hugo leaped from his chair and hopped to the head of the table. He helped his grandmother up from her seat.

"William!" Miss Fannie screeched.

Miss Fannie took William's arm, and together they led Hugo, Courtney, and me out of the dining room. I'm sure a half-dead turtle could have beaten the five of us to the theater. When we got there, we were led to the front row. Hugo stood over Miss Fannie as she settled into a purple rocker.

"Well, Granny, which movie do you recommend for this evening's entertainment?"

"*Planet of the Lavender Women*," Miss Fannie answered without hesitation.

Hugo gave an excited hop. "My favorite! I'll put it on right away." He started toward the projection booth.

"Junior!" Miss Fannie's shrill voice echoed in the theater. "Make the popcorn first!"

In the back of the room was a small snack bar with a popcorn machine. I don't know how I could have missed seeing it before. Courtney was obviously impressed.

"Hugo, do you have any Jujubes?" she asked.

After Hugo plugged in the popcorn machine, he returned with two large boxes of Jujubes. He handed one to Courtney and one to me. While the popcorn was popping, he threaded the projector.

Miss Fannie was in a very talkative mood. "Now, children, you are in for a rare treat."

"You're right, Miss Fannie," Courtney agreed. "These Jujubes are really good."

Miss Fannie frowned at Courtney over the top of her spectacles. "I don't mean that kind of a treat," she snapped. "I'm speaking of my films, young lady. *Planet of the Lavender Women* is a classic. It's the film that made me a star and established my famous trademark—my lavender hair." She patted her purple wig affectionately.

The theater lights dimmed. Just as the words *Planet of the Lavender Women* flashed across the screen, Hugo handed each of us a box of popcorn.

"Junior, did you remember to make mine soggy?"

"Yes, Granny. Two cups of melted butter, just the way you like it." Hugo started to sit down.

"Junior!" Miss Fannie croaked. "The piano! Put a dime in the piano!"

Hugo leaped up and hopped over to a player piano located against the wall beneath Fannie Violet's movie posters. He hurriedly deposited a dime. He hopped back to his chair in perfect time to the ragtime music that filled the room.

Planet of the Lavender Women was probably the first science-fiction movie ever made. The opening scene showed two astronauts lying unconscious beside a demolished spaceship. Both astronauts started coming to at the same time. You could tell they were stunned and in pain. They staggered to their feet. One astronaut was tall and very good-looking. The other one was short and about fifty pounds overweight.

Words flashed across the screen: *Where are we?* When the picture returned, you could tell it was the short, fat astronaut who had asked that question.

The handsome astronaut started moving his lips. Then I read the words, *We've crashed onto an*

*unknown planet on the far side of our galaxy. We're
a million miles from earth!*

It was clear to see that this news really shocked
the short, fat astronaut, but before he could say
anything, the handsome astronaut pointed excitedly
toward some shaking branches in a grove of trees
behind the spaceship.

Suddenly the two men were surrounded by about
twenty gorgeous women, and even though the
movie was in black-and-white, you could tell that
their skin and hair was supposed to be that exotic
color—lavender.

Fannie Violet, the leader of the lavender women,
stepped forward. She wore an animal hide draped
over one shoulder and tied at the waist with the tail
of the same animal.

As the movie progressed, I watched the young
Fannie Violet dash through the woods, leap across a
stream, and grab a vine, Tarzan fashion, to swing
herself up into the entrance of her cave hideout.

Before I knew it, the lights came on. One thing
about silent movies: They're short. *Planet of the
Lavender Women* had lasted only ten minutes.

Hugo woke up William and helped Miss Fannie
to her feet. As he lead them to the door, Courtney
spoke up.

"Hugo", she asked, "can Jan and I stay here for a
while and look at some of my mother's old movies?"

Hugo nodded. "Certainly, Courtney, my young
friend. That is a fine idea. There is a diagram on the

projector, so you should not have any trouble threading the film. However, young ladies"—he frowned and tried to appear stern—"as a child psychiatrist I firmly believe in a proper bedtime for all youngsters. You are to be upstairs and in bed no later than two A.M. Is that agreeable?"

Courtney stifled a giggle and nodded solemnly. "Yes, Hugo. It's agreeable."

As soon as we were left alone, Courtney raced to the projection booth. She smiled broadly, her eyes dancing with anticipation. "Jan, you've probably only seen my mother as that lady reporter on that dumb TV series. Now I'm going to show you my favorite movie." She pulled two large gray cans from the shelf just above her head. I read the title on the cans of film: *Tap Dancing Flight to Romance*.

"That sounds like a musical."

Courtney removed the large reel of film and busied herself trying to thread it onto the projector. "It is a musical. I'll bet you didn't know my mother used to be a singer." She didn't wait for a reply but continued, "Well, this is a great movie, Jan. You're going to love it."

It took Courtney quite a while to adjust the tiny holes in the film properly onto the machine. "Everything's all set," she finally announced. "Jan, go get us some Jujubes and find our seats."

I did as Courtney instructed and had just settled down comfortably in a front-row purple easy chair when Courtney shouted, "Here goes!" Instantly the room was filled with the roar of a lion. The roar was so loud that I'm sure everyone on Fannie Violet's entire island could have heard it. The screen remained dark.

Courtney evidently made the necessary adjustments because, within a few seconds, the lion's picture was on the screen and he was roaring in a normal tone of voice. Courtney sank into a chair next to me and held out her hand for a box of Jujubes.

For the next two hours we were both held captive by Sylvia Sutton. In *Tap Dancing Flight to Romance* she played a stewardess in love with a pilot. At the very end Sylvia and the pilot, plus all the other members of the crew, and even the passengers, sang the title song as they tap-danced their way up the steps of the ramp and onto the plane.

In the final scene the jumbo jet flew into white, fluffy clouds circled by a rainbow. Even though the plane had been swallowed into the clouds and was out of sight, we could still hear the voices of Sylvia and the pilot, loud and clear, above all the voices of the crew and passengers.

We watched two more of Sylvia's movies before we went upstairs to Hugo's old playroom. Courtney turned off the light as we both slid into bed. I heard Courtney choke in the darkness. She hit her pillow twice with her fist.

"There's not much time left, Jan. We've got to get off this stinking island. I'm going to save my mother, and it has to be done before she meets Hugo at six o'clock tomorrow."

For a while we lay quietly, trying to think of some means of escape. Then, five minutes before Hugo's curfew, we both fell sound asleep.

nine

EVEN though we had gone to bed late, Courtney and I awoke early enough to arrive at breakfast at Miss Fannie's scheduled time. I had barely started eating when Courtney took a final gulp of orange juice and dabbed at her mouth with a napkin. "Could we please be excused now, Miss Fannie?" she asked.

I could tell Courtney was very anxious to leave, so I put my fork down and pretended to be finished too.

The old lady squinted at Courtney. "My word, girl, you haven't been here five minutes. Why is it that children are always in such a rush?" she asked no one in particular.

When we reached the back porch, I said, "Why were you in such a big hurry to get outside?"

"We don't have much time left." Courtney spoke in a frustrated voice. "I thought if we walked around the island, maybe we could think of something. Maybe we could try swimming the three miles to shore."

"No!" Courtney couldn't mistake my decisive tone. "We agreed yesterday that it's too dangerous. We can't let ourselves do something stupid just because we're starting to feel desperate. Anyway, Courtney, there are low clouds over the island. Even if we were Olympic swimmers, if we got caught in a fog, we'd never make it."

We walked in silence. We were on a new path today, and it approached the gardener's cottage from the rear. There was an old shed built up against a brick wall a few feet from the back of the cottage.

"I wonder what's in there?" Courtney said, starting to circle the ancient structure.

I followed along behind her. The shed had no windows and the door was padlocked.

Courtney fooled around with the lock for several minutes. "I could blow this dump over if I wanted to," she declared.

She didn't blow it over; instead, she gave the door one solid kick. It immediately fell off its hinges. Courtney was as surprised by this as I was. Together we pushed the door open and stepped inside.

It took a moment for our eyes to adjust to the dark

interior. We stepped over an old inner tube and some scraps of canvas. Against the wall was an antique lawn mower and an assortment of garden tools.

We spotted the boat at the same time. It was lying upside down in a corner. Into our minds leaped a new, fresh hope for escape! We looked at each other and without a single word rushed to inspect the boat. It was nothing more than a small, wooden rowboat; at any other time it would have been considered a worthless piece of junk. But now, to Courtney and me, this piece of junk could mean the difference between life and death. We anxiously ran our hands over the wooden bottom and sides, checking for any damage.

"I think it's in perfect shape!" I whispered excitedly.

"Oars! Look for oars, Jan," Courtney whispered back.

We searched every wall, every corner, every inch of the shed. Finally, we sat down on the overturned boat and hung our heads in a disappointment that was so great we were both on the verge of tears.

Suddenly Courtney leaped to her feet. "Get up, Jan!" she ordered.

"What?" I said, not moving.

"Hurry up!"

She grabbed my arm and pulled me up. When I realized what she was doing, I reached down and helped her turn the boat over. And there on the ground was the most beautiful sight I'd ever seen: two oars!

In our relief and anticipation we started to laugh. The euphoria lasted only a moment before we returned to reality.

"Courtney," I said solemnly. "I'm not sure we should try to escape today. Once we're out in the water, we'll lose our sense of direction in this fog."

"I thought of that too," she replied, equally solemn. "But don't worry. I have a plan."

"Courtney." I sighed. "We've already been through one of your plans."

"I know, but this one is going to be different," she said positively.

"How?" I asked.

"This one's going to work."

"Well?" I asked reluctantly, "What is it?"

She removed a penknife from her "drop dead" jeans. At that moment she actually looked like her mother in a scene from one of her newspaper reporter's adventures. Her voice even sounded like Sylvia Sutton's, and for some crazy reason I suddenly had perfect confidence in Courtney.

"I'm going to unscrew the compass from Hugo's boat," she said. "We know Long Island is north, right?" When I nodded, she continued, "The compass will point north, and we'll row in that direction."

It sounded almost too simple, but I agreed with her. We could do it.

We ran back to the speedboat. It took Courtney less than five minutes to unscrew the compass. She handed it to me, and I was about to run back to the shed with it when she stopped me. "Wait, Jan. There's one more thing I have to do here." She unscrewed the gas cap and started shoveling handfuls of sand into the tank.

"She's Sylvia Sutton's daughter all right," I thought.

Fifteen minutes later, we had moved the rowboat, oars, compass, and my TV set to the beach. We looked back at Miss Fannie's house. Only a faint outline of it was visible through the fog.

Together we pushed the boat into the water and climbed aboard. Courtney grabbed the oars, and I sat facing her, clutching the compass to my body. We had figured that it shouldn't take us more than an hour to row the three miles to Long Island.

The fog lay heavy on the water. It was as if we were in the middle of nowhere. Courtney appeared to me as nothing more than a dark shadow, even though she was within arm's length. The only sound was that of the splashing oars and Courtney's panting.

I kept my eyes on the compass and pointed north. Courtney continued to row steadily for twenty minutes. I could tell she was getting tired, but she didn't complain. She panted as she said, "It's a good thing—we have the compass—or we'd be lost out here—forever."

"Let me know when you want me to take over."

"I can last—a few more—minutes."

It was impossible to believe that it was just late morning. The fog was so thick that it covered us like a blanket. We moved slowly northward in the darkness.

"O.K., Jan," Courtney gasped. "You'll have to—take over now."

It was then that disaster struck. I don't know how it happened because we were both being so careful. Courtney, in a crouched position, moved to my end of the boat. Half standing and half kneeling, I waited for her to take my seat. We were transferring the compass when the boat gave an unexpected lurch. My feet slipped from under me, and as I fell backward, the compass popped from my hands and plunged overboard!

Courtney and I dove our hands into the water up to our elbows in a vain attempt to retrieve the compass. It was useless. In the fog we could see nothing, and the weight of the compass would carry it quickly to the bottom of the ocean. In no time since we'd been kidnapped had we known such utter despair. It would take a miracle to save us now.

I took up the oars, but made no attempt to row. "Courtney," I choked. "I'm sorry. I was trying to be so careful—"

"I know, Jan. It was an accident." Her words sounded hollow, her voice empty of all hope.

We drifted aimlessly through the fog, each of us

lost in thought. For the first time, we faced the possibility that we might not make it. One hour turned into two. How far we had drifted or in what direction we had no way of knowing.

I had read that sometimes before a person dies, all the events of her life flash suddenly before her. It wasn't fair, I thought bitterly to myself. I was only twelve years old. What a gyp! If I was to experience a flashback, it would be short and very boring.

Courtney spoke for the first time in an hour. "Do you know what the passengers on the *Titanic* did as their ship was sinking?"

"Courtney! I don't want to discuss the *Titanic* right now."

"They sang. It helped them keep up their courage."

"I don't feel like singing right now, Courtney."

After a long while, she spoke again. "What time is it now, Jan?"

I had been looking at my watch about every three minutes for the past two and a half hours. I looked again. "Two-thirty," I replied.

Thirty more minutes crept by. Suddenly we became aware of a change in the current and a new sound, as if something huge was moving in the water near us. The waves became rougher, and the rowboat started to pitch from side to side. Miraculously, at that instant, a hole appeared in the fog! Ahead we could see a patch of sunlight. The patch opened wider and revealed a gigantic ocean liner not more than one hundred yards from us! I pulled on the oars with all my strength while Courtney stood up and screamed like a banshee.

"Stop that ship," she demanded, waving her arms wildly about. "We're over here."

I kept rowing as fast as my arms could move.

Courtney kept screaming, "I said, 'Stop that ship'. We're over here!" She took a deep breath and yelled at the top of her lungs, "I said—" Courtney stopped suddenly. "Jan!" she shrieked and started hopping around the rowboat. "Jan! They see us!"

We both became hysterical. I threw down the oars and joined Courtney in her cheerleader routine. The ocean liner was making a wide turn and circling back to pick us up. We hugged each other. Half laughing, half crying, we jumped up and down in our combined relief and excitement. We impatiently watched the ship draw closer.

"You know," I said gleefully, "I think I feel like singing now, Courtney."

ten

O<small>NCE</small> on board ship, we were taken to the captain's quarters. He recognized Courtney and immediately contacted the FBI on the ship's radio.

Thirty minutes later, an FBI helicopter arrived to whisk us to Manhattan. We landed at the United Nations Plaza and were transferred to a police-escorted limousine. Red lights flashing and sirens blaring, we sped toward the Fifth Avenue Central Park Tower. As we pulled up to the curb, flashbulbs started exploding from all directions. Reporters crowded around us, and FBI agents rushed us inside. We shot up to the penthouse in Mrs. Van Allen's private elevator.

When the elevator doors opened, the first people I saw were my parents and Aunt Harry. Just before my mother crushed me tightly to her, I caught a glimpse of Courtney's grandmother. She was shaking her head and dabbing at her swollen, red eyes with a handkerchief. I knew then that Sylvia Sutton wasn't there to greet Courtney.

As much as I cared about Courtney and about her mother's safety, my happiness at seeing my own mother was so great that for the moment I forgot everything else. My eyes filled with tears of relief and joy.

My mother was crying, too. She held me and repeated over and over again, "Jan—Jan—oh, Jan."

It was comforting to know that at last someone remembered my name.

Soon my mother transferred me to my father's strong arms, and I started to cry all over again.

Aunt Harry waited patiently until my father released me. She smiled through misty eyes as I went to her. She hugged me tightly and said, "My pet, thank God you're safe and sound."

It was a moment before my family and I realized how alone Courtney and Mrs. Van Allen were. The nightmare hadn't ended for them yet.

Mrs. Van Allen said through a hiccup, "Why don't we all go inside?" She dabbed at her eyes with a handkerchief covered with about a pound of mascara, rouge, and wrinkle cream. What was left of her makeup was streaked all over her face.

My mother went to Courtney's side and wrapped an arm around her shoulders. She gave Courtney a reassuring smile. "Courtney, honey," she said, "the FBI called just before you got here. They told us we should have word about your parents any minute now."

Courtney nodded gratefully and let my mother lead her into the Van Allen apartment. We were followed inside by two FBI agents.

We found seats in the living room and started to talk in hushed tones. All but Aunt Harry, that is.

"Children," she said, "I want you to know that this maniac, Hugo Malcalm, is going to get what he deserves. I personally will see to it."

Courtney and I stared at Aunt Harry.

"Mrs. Petrie," Courtney said, "how did you know it was Hugo who kidnapped Jan and me?"

"We didn't until this afternoon when he telephoned your mother to set up their meeting," Aunt Harry replied.

"Your mother, bless her heart," Mrs. Van Allen hiccupped into her handkerchief, "wanted to go to meet Hugo by herself as he demanded. But your father, bless his heart too"—Mrs. Van Allen hiccupped again—"insisted on going with her. Then the FBI, bless their hearts, insisted on following them both. So you see, Courtney, my sweet, everything is going to be just fine." With the conclusion of this speech, Mrs. Van Allen collapsed into tears and buried her face into her much used handkerchief.

With her grandmother practically hysterical, it

was clear that Courtney was more worried than ever.

My father's voice was steady and confident. "Courtney, the FBI has your parents under constant surveillance. When they called here a little while ago, they said they'd followed them into Dr. Malcolm's office on Park Avenue. They have the building surrounded by policemen."

"Dad," I said, "nobody calls Hugo Dr. Malcolm."

"What do you mean, honey?" my father asked.

I was about to explain all about Hugo's first-name theory when we heard a commotion in the corridor. Courtney slid to the edge of her chair, and for a second no one breathed.

The front door opened, and Sylvia Sutton entered, followed by the senator. Sylvia was dressed perfectly, and every blond hair was in place, exactly like when she appears on television as the LA lady reporter. Her dazzling smile was the same one I'd seen hundreds of times on TV—only this time it was meant for Courtney alone.

Courtney flew into her mother's opened arms.

"Courtney, darling," Sylvia cried.

For a long moment, Courtney and her mother held each other as if they'd never let go. When at last they did, Courtney received the same welcome from the senator.

Sylvia turned her radiant smile toward my family. "Susan, Ben, Mrs. Petrie, thank you for staying here with Courtney. We do appreciate—"

Courtney, still clinging to her father's hand, interrupted, "Mom, I was really worried about you."

Sylvia was touched by her daughter's concern. She cupped Courtney's face between her hands and said in that familiar, husky voice, "Courtney, *you* were the one who was kidnapped. We were all worried sick about you and—" Those famous blue eyes lifted from Courtney's eyes and stared right into mine. She hesitated for a moment, then said, "Jan."

Sylvia Sutton remembered my name! I smiled back at her, and I knew then that even if I lived to be as old as Fannie Violet, Sylvia Sutton would always be my favorite actress.

"But, Mom," Courtney said, "it was really you that Hugo wanted to kidnap. He wanted to keep you in his private theater along with all your old posters and movies."

"No, my young friend." Every head in the room jerked in the direction of the doorway. There stood Hugo, handcuffed to an FBI agent! Hugo shook his head, "You do not understand. I only wanted to meet your mother. I am her greatest fan, that is true." He looked admiringly at his idol before continuing. "I would never wish to harm her. I simply wanted her to read my play."

Hugo took a hop forward. The unexpected movement was such a shock to the FBI agent handcuffed to him that he fell to his knees before he was able to recover his balance.

Aunt Harry glared at Hugo and declared loudly, "I don't understand what that idiot is doing here!"

"Hugo, how did you get off the island?" Courtney asked.

Hugo smiled at her. "Nobody put sand in the gas tank of the Miss Fannie, my young friend."

"The FBI wants to get everyone's statement at the same time," Senator Van Allen cut in.

"That's correct, senator," said one of the agents. "I am sorry, folks," he apologized to everyone in the room, "but this shouldn't take long."

"You see," Hugo said to everyone in general, "my play is a great work of art, and it was written especially for Sylvia."

Hugo took another hop forward. The agent at his side crashed to his knees again. When he regained his balance, he gave Hugo a dirty look and planted his feet squarely on the floor.

When their equipment was set up, the agents started taking down what they considered to be important information. After nearly an hour, they started to gather up tape recorders, notebooks, a bugging device from one of the phones, and Hugo.

"Thank you for your time," the head agent said. "We'll take Dr. Malcalm into headquarters for further questioning, but I think we'll all agree that he is going to need a great deal of psychiatric care."

Hugo started to take another hop, but this time the agent was ready. Hugo's arm was practically jerked off as he fell backward onto the floor. With an embarrassed giggle, he said, "I have to admit, I'm going to hate having to see a psychiatrist. They're all a bunch of crackpots!"

"While Jim and I were in Hugo's office," Sylvia said kindly, "we had time to read a part of Hugo's play. It's a drama about a singing trapeze artist who falls in love with a circus horse." She smiled at Hugo. "Perhaps now you'll have more time to work some of the bugs out of the play, Hugo."

Hugo smiled gratefully at Sylvia, and Courtney and I said good-bye to him as he got up and hopped to the door behind the FBI agent.

Before my family returned to Aunt Harry's apartment, I was able to tell Sylvia Sutton how much I enjoyed her series. She answered all my questions about her TV character, her studio, and Hollywood.

Courtney's father was very nice too. He promised my parents he'd give us a special tour of the capital if we were ever in Washington.

It was getting late and we were about to leave the Van Allen apartment when the butler entered. He spoke directly to Senator Van Allen. "The President is on the phone, sir."

The senator took the call in the living room. A hush fell over the room as we listened to him say, "Mr. President? Yes, sir, she's just fine . . . thank you, Mr. President. One moment, I'll put her on the line." Courtney's father held one hand over the receiver and looked fondly at her. "Honey, it's the President. He wants to speak to you."

Courtney beamed happily as she lifted the receiver to her ear. I waited to hear her say, "Pass the salt, please," but she didn't. She nodded once or twice and said, "Thank you," very politely. Then she held the phone toward me and said, "Jan, the President wants to talk to you, too."

I looked at my parents and Aunt Harry. Everyone watched me as I nervously took the phone from Courtney.

"Hello," I said.

From the other end a familiar voice said, "Hello, you must be Jan Travis."

I couldn't believe it! The President of the United States knew my name! "Yes, sir," I replied as calmly as I could.

"I'd like you to know how happy I am that you and Courtney are safe at home."

"Thank you, sir," I replied.

"I understand that you live in California. Before you return to your home, I hope you'll come with Courtney and her family and have lunch with me here at the White House one day next week."

"I'll have to ask my parents."

The President laughed. "You do that, Jan. I hope to see you next week."

"Thank you, Mr. President. Good-bye." I shakily hung up the receiver.

eleven

THE following afternoon I was in Courtney's room reading the latest edition of the morning newspapers. The front page was covered with news of our escape. There were pictures of the two of us climbing out of the FBI helicopter. There were more pictures showing us being herded into the Fifth Avenue Central Park Tower.

With Hugo's cooperation, the FBI had been led to Miss Fannie's island. Shortly before midnight, Denise had been taken into custody. On the second page there were two pictures of Miss Fannie. One had been taken sixty-three years ago when she had been Hollywood's most glamorous silent-screen star. The second picture showed Miss Fannie and William seated on a couch in the living room of her island estate while being questioned by the FBI.

Miss Fannie appeared to be adjusting her wig. William was sleeping.

The story beneath the pictures said that Fannie Violet and William were not suspects in the Courtney Van Allen kidnapping. It also quoted Miss Fannie as saying that she would consider coming out of retirement to return to the screen if she was offered the right role. (A later edition of the newspaper reported that a film producer had called to offer Miss Fannie the role of Violet O'Hara, Scarlett's great-grandmother, in a remake of *Gone With the Wind!*)

After we had read and reread all the papers spread on the floor in front of us, Courtney turned on the conclusion of *King Kong Eats Chinatown.* I had brought along the diary that Aunt Harry had given me. I chewed thoughtfully on the end of a ballpoint pen as I watched King Kong bite off the top of a giant pagoda.

Courtney stretched out on the rug in front of the TV set. In place of her "drop dead" outfit she was wearing pale blue pants and a matching blouse. Her hair, now a shining yellow, fell across her shoulders. She really did look like her mother.

As we watched King Kong devour Chinatown, one building at a time, Courtney said, "Jan, did I tell you I'm going back to California with my parents? All three of us are going to be living together again when my father isn't in Washington on business."

I smiled. "That's the third time you've told me today."

Courtney laughed. "I talked to my parents, and they said I should invite you to our ranch. There's a lot of things to do near where I live, Jan. If we get tired of the swimming pool and tennis courts, we can always go horseback riding, sail over to Catalina, go to the studio and watch my mom film her series, or spend a few days at Disneyland."

"Could we really do all those things?" I asked, excited at the prospect.

"Sure," Courtney replied. "I mean, after all we've been through together, Jan, I think we should always remain good friends."

"I think so too, Courtney," I agreed happily.

After a while, Courtney turned her attention back to King Kong, and I started to write in my diary.

Dear Diary, I want to tell you about an unusual adventure I had recently. . . .